The Friendship Tree

Diversity, Equality, and Inclusion

Isaac Lewis

Published by Whimsy Tales Press, 2024.

This is a work of fiction. Similarities to real people, places, or events are entirely coincidental.

THE FRIENDSHIP TREE

First edition. November 20, 2024.

Copyright © 2024 Isaac Lewis.

ISBN: 979-8227706317

Written by Isaac Lewis.

Table of Contents

Preface 1
Chapter 1: The Big Idea 2
Chapter 2: Gathering the Soil 6
Chapter 3: The Planting Ceremony 10
Chapter 4: Naming the Tree 14
Chapter 5: Building a Tree Garden 18
Chapter 6: The Tree's First Bloom 22
Chapter 7: Seasons of Change 26
Chapter 8: Protecting the Tree 30
Chapter 9: The Friendship Tree Festival 35
Chapter 10: A Lesson in Patience 39
Chapter 11: Roots Run Deep 43
Chapter 12: A Year in Reflection 47
Chapter 13: Adapting to Challenges 52
Chapter 14: Celebrating Differences 56
Chapter 15: Facing Difficult Choices 60
Chapter 16: Planting New Seeds 65
Chapter 17: The Gift of Passing It On 70
Chapter 18: A Lesson in Letting Go 74
Chapter 19: The Circle Reunited 78
Chapter 20: Seasons of Friendship 82
Chapter 21: A New Seed 85
Chapter 22: The Tree of Many Stories 90
Chapter 23: A Legacy Renewed 94
Chapter 24: Seeds of the Future 98
Chapter 25: The Tree's Endless Reach 103

Preface

The Friendship Tree grew from a simple idea: that a friendship, like a tree, can be planted, cared for, and cherished over time, until its roots stretch deep and its branches touch many lives. This story follows the journey of four friends as they plant a sapling, each bringing soil from their homeland, and care for it together. Through their joys, challenges, and adventures, the tree becomes more than a symbol; it becomes a part of the community's heart, a gathering place, and a source of inspiration. The Friendship Tree shows how our roots connect us and reminds us that true friendship grows across generations. This book is an invitation to celebrate kindness, respect, and the beauty of shared lives. We hope it touches your heart as much as it has ours.

Chapter 1: The Big Idea

In the heart of a bustling town, nestled among tall buildings and wide streets, lay a small park. This wasn't just any park; it was a special gathering place for children from all walks of life. Though their houses might have looked different, and their families spoke in a range of accents, the children who played here came together every afternoon. On this particular sunny day, the air hummed with an extra touch of excitement.

In a shaded corner of the park, a group of children had gathered to sit on the cool grass, their faces lit with excitement and curiosity. It wasn't every day that a big idea would sprout among them, but they all felt it stirring as they exchanged glances, as if sensing that something magical was about to unfold.

As the children spoke and laughed together, it was clear that they each came from a unique background. Some wore clothes with intricate patterns, others brought along small snacks that carried unfamiliar but delightful scents, and all of them had stories to tell, stories that were as different as the places they called home. They had all been coming to this park for as long as they could remember, playing games and getting to know each other. Over time, they realized that while they each had their own favorite games, stories, and traditions, what truly mattered was the joy they shared.

On this particular day, one child named Elara, who was known for her big ideas and even bigger imagination, had gathered her friends for a discussion. Elara's eyes sparkled as she spoke, her voice full of wonder. "I was thinking," she began, "What if we plant something together here in the park? Something that's ours, something that grows with us?"

The group fell silent as they pondered this. A few exchanged thoughtful looks, trying to grasp what Elara was suggesting. A boy named Leo, known for always asking questions, squinted his eyes thoughtfully. "Like a tree?" he asked, scratching his head. "But what's so special about a tree? It just stands there. It doesn't even move!"

Elara laughed and nodded, understanding Leo's confusion. "Yes, a tree! But not just any tree. It would be our tree. Imagine that it's like a symbol, a symbol of our friendship, and of all the things that make each of us special. And what if," she paused, building the suspense as her friends leaned in, "we each bring soil from our homes to plant it together? That way, our tree would have a little piece of each of us!"

A buzz of excitement rippled through the group. They began to imagine the possibilities, their minds swirling with ideas about what this tree could mean. A girl named Samira, who loved art and often painted pictures of the places she dreamed of visiting, clasped her hands together with enthusiasm. "That would mean our tree would have all our different stories and memories, right there in the roots! It would be a little piece of home for all of us, no matter where we're from."

The children nodded, each grasping the beauty of the idea. They imagined a tree standing tall, its branches spreading wide like welcoming arms, a part of each of them held in its roots. Elara could hardly contain her excitement, her voice rising as she continued. "And think of it! As the tree grows, we can watch it change and become stronger, just like we do. We could come here together to take care of it and make sure it grows healthy and strong. It would be our responsibility, and we'd be doing it together."

Leo, still skeptical but now curious, asked, "What kind of tree would we plant? Do we all get a say in it?"

Elara smiled, recognizing that everyone's input mattered. "Of course! We'd all choose the tree together. It has to be a tree that means something to all of us."

And so, the children set off on the first step of their big idea. They began to talk about what kind of tree they might plant and the different symbols each tree could represent. They were thrilled by the idea of a tree that could grow with them and hold the many pieces of their stories. They also realized it would need to be a tree that could adapt to all seasons, just like they did. They discussed trees that blossomed with flowers, trees that provided shade, and trees that bore fruit. Each child offered their ideas, reflecting on what the tree could mean for them all.

After a while, they reached a consensus, choosing a tree that was known for its strength, endurance, and ability to grow tall and wide, with branches that could reach out like a big, open hug. It would be the perfect symbol of friendship and unity, just like Elara had imagined.

With their choice made, Elara reminded everyone of the next step in their plan. "We'll all go home tonight and gather a small bit of soil from around our houses. It doesn't have to be much, just a handful. But when we bring it back here, it will be like we're each putting a part of our lives into the tree."

The idea of bringing soil from their homes added a touch of mystery and excitement to the plan. Each child was eager to contribute a bit of the earth from their own surroundings, knowing it would form the foundation for their shared tree. As they parted ways that evening, they all felt a renewed sense of purpose. The park, which had always been a place of games and laughter, now held the promise of something even greater: a living reminder of the friendship they shared and the dreams they would grow together.

The next day, the children returned to the park, each carrying a small container or bag filled with soil. They gathered around the hole they had dug, each one waiting eagerly to add their soil to the mix. They went one by one, taking turns to sprinkle their soil into the hole. Some had soil that was dark and rich, others light and sandy, and still others had soil that held a reddish tint. Each type of soil was different, just like the children who had brought it. But as it all mixed together, it created a new blend, a symbol of their united effort and the diversity within their friendship.

As the last handful of soil was added, they gently placed the sapling in the hole, packing the earth around it with care. They stood back, feeling a deep sense of pride and connection to the tiny tree that now stood before them. Though it was just a small sapling, the children saw it as a symbol of the big dreams they held for their friendship and their future together.

After they finished planting the tree, they gathered in a circle around it. Elara spoke up once more, her voice soft but filled with determination. "This tree is our promise to each other. Just like it will need sunlight, water, and care to grow strong, our friendship needs kindness, understanding, and respect. We'll come here often, take care of it together, and make sure it grows big and strong."

Chapter 2: Gathering the Soil

Each child left the park that day with a renewed sense of excitement and purpose. Their minds were buzzing with thoughts about the tree they had planted together and the soil they'd contributed. It was amazing to think that something as simple as soil, a little piece of the earth they came from, could represent so much. Each handful was a connection to their homes, their families, and the places that made them who they were. It was like taking a piece of their identity and sharing it with each other, all to help their new tree grow.

As they walked home, each child thought about where they would gather the soil. Some wanted to take it from a favorite place in their yard, somewhere they had played or watched flowers bloom in spring. Others wanted to gather soil from spots with meaning to their families, places that held stories passed down by their parents and grandparents. Every one of them had a different idea about where to find the soil, but all of them knew that they wanted to find just the right spot.

Leo, who was always curious and loved exploring, couldn't wait to get home. His family's yard was filled with plants and bushes his mom had been nurturing for years. She loved her garden, and every plant had its own story. Leo decided he would collect soil from under the big rose bush that grew near his back porch. He remembered his mom telling him that his grandmother had planted the first rose bush in their family's yard when she was young, passing down cuttings to each new home they moved to. Leo's mom kept the tradition alive, and now the roses bloomed brightly every year. To him, the soil under the rose bush was a piece of his family's history, a bit of love and care handed down through generations.

When Leo explained his plan to his mom, she smiled warmly, understanding why he wanted to take soil from such a special place. She handed him a small spade and watched as he carefully dug a handful of soil, placing it in a small container. As he scooped the soil, he could feel a sense of pride and connection to his family's legacy. He knew his soil would be part of something even bigger now, blending with the soil his friends would bring.

In a different part of town, Elara was having her own adventure. Her family lived near a small lake where she loved to play with her younger siblings. She had always found a special comfort by the water, feeling a connection to nature and its quiet beauty. Elara decided she wanted to gather her soil from the lake's edge, where the earth was cool and moist. She imagined how the soil there held memories of long summer days spent skipping stones and watching the ripples stretch across the water. Her dad walked with her down to the lake, a quiet smile on his face as he saw the excitement in her eyes.

As she dug into the soft ground, Elara thought about how much the lake meant to her. She whispered a small promise to herself to return often, to remember where she came from even as she shared it with others. She could hardly wait to see her soil mix with her friends', knowing that her special memories would blend with theirs.

Meanwhile, Samira, who adored art and creativity, was preparing to gather her soil in a different way. Her home was a little apartment on the second floor of a cozy building, surrounded by flower boxes and potted plants her family kept on their balcony. Samira loved watching her mother tend to these plants every morning, caring for them with gentle hands. To Samira, those flower boxes were more than just containers for plants—they were symbols of hope and resilience. Even though they lived in a busy neighborhood with little space, her mother's plants had managed to thrive.

With her mother's help, Samira carefully loosened the soil from one of their flower boxes, scooping it into a small cloth bag. She thought about how this soil represented her family's ability to grow and thrive no matter where they were, bringing beauty to the world even in small spaces. As she held the bag in her hands, Samira imagined the tree in the park growing tall, just like the plants on her balcony. She hoped it would carry the same strength and beauty, a reminder that even small things could make a big difference.

Nearby, Liam was thinking hard about where to find his soil. His family had moved around a lot, and he didn't feel a strong connection to any particular spot in his backyard. But as he looked out the window, he spotted the old oak tree by the corner of the fence. He remembered playing there, pretending the branches were arms reaching out to protect him. It was a spot where he often sat and thought, a place where he felt safe and grounded. With a little smile, he decided that this would be the perfect spot for his soil.

He crouched by the tree, feeling the rough bark under his fingers as he dug a small scoop of soil. His mind drifted to memories of climbing the oak, of the times he had sat beneath it with a book, lost in stories that took him to distant lands. This tree had been his friend, in a way, and now he would share a part of it with the Friendship Tree.

As each child gathered their soil, they felt a mix of emotions. They realized that while soil was something ordinary, something they usually walked over without a second thought, it held a deeper meaning now. It was a reminder of home, of love and connection, of memories both big and small. And as they prepared to bring their soil to the park, they knew they were sharing something truly special with each other.

The next day, the children gathered at the park, each carrying their container of soil, cradling it as if it were a precious treasure. They sat in a circle, showing their soil to one another, marveling at the different colors and textures. Some soil was dark and rich, others light and sandy, some even held tiny stones and bits of leaves. Each handful was unique, like the children themselves.

Elara, her eyes shining with excitement, explained how she had chosen the soil from the lake's edge. She described the calmness of the water and the peace she felt there, sharing her hopes that the tree would carry that sense of calm. Leo followed, talking about the roses and the legacy they represented. Samira shared her story of resilience, of her mother's flower boxes and the beauty they created in a small space. And Liam, with a shy smile, told them about the old oak tree, the friend who had been with him through all his adventures.

As each child spoke, they listened closely, understanding that each story added something special to their project. They could see the roots of their friendship growing deeper, intertwined with the soil they held in their hands. In a quiet way, they realized they were learning more about each other, discovering pieces of their friends they hadn't known before.

Once everyone had shared their stories, they moved to the little sapling they had planted. One by one, they poured their soil around the tree's base, watching as the different soils mixed and blended together. In that moment, they felt a sense of awe. It was as if their lives had joined, becoming part of something greater than themselves. They were no longer just children playing in the park; they were caretakers of a shared dream, a promise to nurture this tree and the friendship it symbolized.

Chapter 3: The Planting Ceremony

The day dawned bright and clear, with a sky painted in soft shades of blue and whispers of clouds drifting lazily across. It was the perfect day for a celebration, a day the children had eagerly awaited since they first planted the idea of the Friendship Tree. The morning air was filled with the sounds of birds singing from nearby trees, and a gentle breeze swept through the park, rustling the grass and filling the space with a sense of calm and anticipation. Today, they would finally come together to hold a special ceremony, not just to plant a tree, but to plant a piece of themselves, a promise to each other, and a hope for the future.

One by one, the children arrived at the park, each carrying a container of soil. Some had chosen small jars, while others had brought little bags or even tiny wooden boxes filled with the earth they'd carefully collected from home. The sight of these containers brought a sense of magic and mystery to the day, each one holding stories and memories that only they knew. They walked to the chosen spot where their sapling stood waiting, its leaves gently swaying in the morning light. It was a small, sturdy tree, but to the children, it was already mighty, holding within it all their dreams and friendships.

Elara was the first to arrive, her face glowing with excitement as she saw the tree standing proudly in the center of their circle. She set down her little bag of soil and gently touched one of the leaves, whispering a quiet hello to the sapling as if it could understand her. Soon after, Leo appeared, balancing his container with care and waving to Elara with a grin. "Ready for the big day?" he asked, his voice full of enthusiasm. Elara nodded, her eyes sparkling. "More than ready! Today, it really feels like our dream is coming true."

As the others arrived, each carrying their soil, the circle around the tree grew larger and livelier. They exchanged hugs and high-fives, their excitement blending into a shared energy that filled the air. Samira, holding her soil with both hands, looked around at her friends and said, "It's amazing, isn't it? We're really doing something special today, something that will last for a long, long time." The others nodded in agreement, feeling the weight of her words and the significance of the moment. Today was more than just an ordinary day—it was the beginning of something extraordinary.

When everyone was gathered, Elara took a step forward, clearing her throat as she began to speak. "Today, we're not just planting a tree. We're planting a part of ourselves. Each of us has brought soil from our homes, from places that mean something to us. We're mixing our soil together because, just like this tree, our friendship grows stronger when we come together." Her words were met with nods and smiles, a quiet understanding passing through the group. They knew that they weren't just helping a tree grow; they were creating a foundation for their friendship that would grow and change just as they would.

After a moment, Leo stepped forward, lifting his container of soil with a grin. "Alright, let's do this! I say we each take a turn adding our soil and saying something to the tree. It can be anything—a wish, a hope, a promise." The others agreed, feeling that this would make the ceremony even more meaningful. They arranged themselves in a small circle around the tree, their containers of soil held close as if protecting something precious.

Elara went first, gently opening her bag of soil and kneeling next to the tree. She scooped a handful of the earth and let it fall around the sapling's roots. "I hope you grow strong and tall," she whispered to the tree. "I hope you're a reminder to us that friendship needs care, kindness, and patience. And I hope we remember to come here and watch you grow." As she stood up, the group gave her a little cheer, and she stepped back with a smile, feeling a warmth spread through her as she joined her friends in the circle.

Next, Samira stepped forward, holding her small cloth bag carefully. She took a deep breath, her eyes shining with a mix of excitement and thoughtfulness. "This soil is from the flowers on my balcony," she began, sprinkling it gently around the base of the tree. "It's a reminder that even small things can grow and make the world a more beautiful place. I hope this tree will show us that no matter where we come from, we can grow together." Her words were met with a soft murmur of agreement, and she stepped back with a quiet smile, feeling the strength of her wish take root.

Leo followed, holding his jar of soil with a look of pride. As he knelt by the tree, he let the soil trickle from his fingers and said, "This is from the rose bush my grandma planted a long time ago. It reminds me that family is important, and even when things change, we still have our roots. I hope this tree reminds us of that." His words were simple but carried a weight that the others felt deeply, and they gave him a round of applause as he returned to his spot in the circle.

One by one, each child came forward, sharing their soil and their thoughts with the tree. Some spoke about family, others about friendship, and some simply made wishes for happiness and kindness. Each handful of soil added a piece of their world to the growing foundation, a blend of memories, dreams, and promises that would nourish the tree and, in a way, each other. It was a ceremony filled with warmth and laughter, but also a sense of wonder, as if they were creating something sacred, something that held a piece of their souls.

When every last bit of soil had been added around the sapling, they gathered close, admiring the tree as it stood surrounded by their mixed soils, each one rich with stories and meaning. They could see tiny stones, flecks of leaves, and bits of root peeking through the soil, reminders of the unique journeys that had brought them together. For a moment, they simply stood there in silence, feeling the presence of the tree and the bond they had created. It was as if the tree had woven their lives together, creating something new and beautiful that would only grow stronger with time.

After a moment, Elara spoke up. "Let's make a promise to come here often, to take care of the tree and each other. And let's promise to keep adding to this soil, with our stories and memories, so that it always has a part of us." The group nodded in agreement, their faces lit with a mixture of joy and determination. They felt the weight of her words, understanding that they were not just promising to care for a tree but to care for each other, to be there through the seasons of life, no matter where they might go.

With a final cheer, they placed their hands together, forming a circle around the tree as they looked at each other, their hearts full of pride and a sense of belonging. It was a moment they would remember forever, a moment where they became more than friends—they became caretakers of something larger than themselves. They felt as if they had planted a part of their hearts in that park, creating a legacy that would endure through the years, just as the tree would.

Chapter 4: Naming the Tree

It had been a few days since the children held their planting ceremony, and every one of them was eager to return to the park to see their tree. After school, they ran to the park with excitement and curiosity. As they approached, they were pleased to see their sapling standing tall in the sunlight, looking as if it had already grown a little since they last saw it. Seeing the tree gave them a feeling of accomplishment, a reminder that their friendship and efforts had created something that would continue to grow and thrive.

Gathering around the tree, they felt a sense of pride, but they also felt that something was missing. They had mixed their soil, made wishes, and even promised to take care of the tree, but it still felt incomplete. There was a shared sense that this tree, now such an important part of their lives, needed a name. Just like each of them had names that told something about who they were, the tree needed one too. It felt strange to keep calling it simply "the tree" or "our tree" when it had come to mean so much more.

It was Elara who voiced what everyone was thinking. "Our tree needs a name," she said, her voice soft but filled with conviction. "I mean, it's special to us, right? It's like a part of our friendship, so it should have a name that reflects that." The others nodded in agreement, each of them feeling the same way. They wanted a name that would honor what the tree stood for and remind them of everything they shared.

Leo, who loved thinking out loud and always had plenty of ideas, jumped right in. "How about we name it something cool, like... Unity Tree? Or maybe Friendship Oak? Something that sounds strong!" His face lit up as he listed off names, each one more enthusiastic than the last. But while some of his suggestions sounded impressive, the others didn't feel like they quite captured the heart of what the tree meant to them.

Samira, who always saw things from a creative perspective, closed her eyes for a moment, thinking deeply. "I think the name should be something that sounds gentle and welcoming," she suggested. "This tree isn't just about being strong; it's also about being a place where we all feel safe and happy. It should be something that makes us feel at home."

Hearing this, the children grew thoughtful. They all had their own ideas about what the tree's name should mean. Elara wanted a name that reflected their shared dreams, Leo wanted something bold and powerful, and Samira wanted a name that captured the tree's warmth and kindness. It quickly became clear that everyone had a different idea of what the tree represented. And as the children continued to share suggestions, they realized that choosing the perfect name would be harder than they had expected.

After a while, they decided to take a break from brainstorming and split into smaller groups to discuss ideas. Leo and Elara sat down on a nearby bench, trying to come up with names that combined their love for adventure and strength. They threw around ideas like "Journey Tree" and "Explorer," each one sparking a new idea but none quite fitting. Meanwhile, Samira sat with Liam, who was known for being thoughtful and calm, quietly discussing names that reflected a sense of peace and unity. They liked the idea of calling the tree something like "Harmony" or "Peaceful Root," but they weren't sure if it captured everything they wanted.

As the afternoon passed, the children started to feel frustrated. They had so many ideas, but every time they thought they had found the perfect name, someone would feel it didn't quite fit. Each suggestion was meaningful in its own way, but the tree was all of those things and more. They realized that naming something as special as their tree was not an easy task, especially when each of them saw it from a slightly different perspective.

Finally, Elara spoke up, her voice filled with determination. "Why don't we try this? We all know the tree means something different to each of us, but maybe we can think about it in a way that includes everyone's ideas. Let's make a list of all the things this tree stands for, then we can use that to find a name that combines everything."

The group agreed that this was a good idea, and they took out a notebook and started writing down words that described what the tree meant to them. They wrote words like "friendship," "growth," "strength," "peace," "home," "dreams," and "love." The list quickly grew long, each word adding a new layer of meaning to the tree. As they looked at the words together, they realized that their tree was more than just a plant—it was a symbol of all the things they held dear.

With the list in front of them, the children tried to mix and match words, coming up with combinations that captured as many meanings as possible. They thought of names like "Unity Grove," "Dream Tree," and "Forever Oak." Each name felt closer to what they wanted, but they still couldn't settle on the perfect choice. They began to understand that no single word could capture everything their tree represented, and that was okay. What mattered was that they were doing this together, putting their hearts into finding a name that reflected all the different pieces of their friendship.

As the sun began to set, casting a warm glow over the park, Samira looked at the tree and suddenly had an idea. "What if we call it the 'Friendship Tree'? I know it sounds simple, but isn't that really what this tree is? It's about us being friends, about bringing everything we are together and letting it grow into something beautiful. Sometimes, the simplest names are the best because they say exactly what's in our hearts."

The others looked at each other, feeling the truth in Samira's words. They had spent all day trying to find the perfect name, but maybe the answer had been there all along. "Friendship Tree" felt right because it didn't need to be fancy or complicated; it was simply the truth. This tree was a symbol of their friendship, and its name would remind them of that every time they saw it.

Elara nodded, her face breaking into a smile. "I love it. It's perfect. It's exactly what this tree is—a symbol of our friendship, simple and real." The rest of the group agreed, their hearts lifting with a sense of relief and satisfaction. They knew that "Friendship Tree" might not have been the most elaborate name, but it was the truest one. And sometimes, truth was all that was needed.

With their decision made, they gathered in a circle around the tree, feeling a renewed connection to it now that it had a name. The Friendship Tree stood as a testament to their bond, its roots growing deeper with every moment they spent together. They promised to visit often, to care for it, and to remember the journey that had led them to this point. For them, this wasn't just the end of a naming ceremony—it was the beginning of a shared commitment to nurture the Friendship Tree and to keep their friendship alive and strong.

Chapter 5: Building a Tree Garden

It was a bright Saturday morning when the children met at the park, gathering once again around their Friendship Tree. Now that it had a name and a special meaning to each of them, the tree felt even more alive, as if it were part of their group, a quiet listener to all their laughter, secrets, and dreams. They had visited it every day since naming it, and each time, they noticed new details about it—the way its leaves caught the sunlight, the tiny shoots beginning to grow from its base, and even how the soil around it had already started to settle from where they had poured their soils together. Their Friendship Tree felt like it was growing stronger, and so was their dedication to caring for it.

As they gathered around, Leo, always full of ideas and energy, bounced on his heels with a grin. "Our tree's doing great, but don't you think it looks a bit lonely?" he asked, casting a thoughtful look around the empty ground surrounding the tree. The other kids tilted their heads, noticing the bare earth surrounding the Friendship Tree. It was just dirt stretching out in all directions, and Leo was right—it looked as though something was missing. The tree was full of potential and beauty, but it needed a place that could reflect everything it meant to them.

Samira's eyes sparkled as she thought aloud, "What if we made a garden around it? Not just any garden, but a special one with things that each of us brings? Then our tree wouldn't be alone—it would be surrounded by little pieces of us, just like the soil we added." Her idea sparked excitement among the others, who immediately started imagining what they could add to this new garden. They envisioned a colorful, vibrant space that would represent the diversity and unity of their friendship, a space that would grow and change as they did.

Elara clapped her hands together in delight. "That's a perfect idea! Let's make it a special garden, one that tells a story. We can bring things from home, things that mean something to us, and place them around the tree. That way, our tree garden will be like a little world of memories, dreams, and things we love." The group agreed enthusiastically, inspired by the thought of creating a place that represented them all, where each item would tell a piece of their story.

Excited by the plan, they decided to return the following weekend to bring their contributions. In the days that followed, each child thought carefully about what they would add to the garden. They wanted to bring something meaningful, something that captured a little part of themselves, and that would add to the magic and beauty of their shared space.

The following Saturday arrived, and the children returned to the park, each carrying a small object wrapped carefully or tucked safely in their backpacks. They were brimming with anticipation, each child excited to reveal their addition to the garden. The space around the Friendship Tree had been cleared a bit, with a ring of stones the children had gathered from around the park marking the boundary of their new garden. It was a blank canvas, waiting for them to fill it with memories and treasures.

Elara went first, carefully unwrapping a small glass prism that caught the sunlight and scattered it into rainbow colors. She held it up, showing it to her friends, who watched in awe as the light danced in tiny rainbows on the ground. "This was a gift from my grandmother," she explained. "She told me it's a reminder that even a single beam of light can create beautiful things if you look at it the right way. I thought it would be perfect for our garden, to remind us to always see the beauty in things." She placed the prism near the base of the tree, where it would catch the sunlight during the day, filling their garden with little bursts of color.

Samira went next, pulling out a small painted rock she had made herself. It was decorated with swirling patterns in bright, cheerful colors, with a tiny heart in the center. She smiled shyly as she explained,

"I made this rock because I love painting and colors. The patterns represent all the twists and turns of life, and the heart is for all the people I care about. I thought it would bring happiness and color to our garden." She placed the rock beside Elara's prism, and the others admired how the colors and patterns added warmth and personality to their growing space.

Leo, always thinking practically, had brought a small bottle filled with seeds from the roses in his backyard. He held it up proudly, shaking the bottle so they could hear the tiny seeds rattling inside. "These are from my mom's rose bushes," he said. "If we plant them here, they'll grow into roses that bloom every year. It'll remind us of my grandma and my family, and it'll mean we're adding something that will keep growing with the tree." The group agreed it was a wonderful idea, and they decided to plant the seeds in a small patch beside the tree, hoping that one day, beautiful roses would bloom, adding to the life and beauty of their garden.

Liam, quiet but thoughtful, revealed his contribution next. He had brought a smooth, round stone he had found by the river near his house, where he often went to think or read. He explained softly, "This stone reminds me of the river and the calm it brings me. I thought it could bring a sense of peace to our garden, like a little piece of the river that stays with us." He placed the stone gently near the base of the tree, where it added a grounded, serene touch to the garden.

The children continued to add their pieces, each one as unique as the person who brought it. Some added tiny wooden carvings or small decorations, each with a story or memory tied to it. A few even brought flowers they planted in little patches, adding splashes of color that would grow and bloom with the seasons. As each item found its place around the tree, the garden began to take shape, transforming from a bare patch of earth into a vibrant, living space filled with meaning.

With every addition, the children saw how their garden became more than just a collection of objects. It was a place where their memories and stories intertwined, where every piece told a story of who they were and what they cared about. As they stepped back to admire their work, they felt a deep sense of connection—not just to the Friendship Tree, but to each other. The garden had become a living symbol of their bond, a place that represented all their dreams, values, and hopes.

After everything was in place, they took a step back to look at the garden they had created. The area around the Friendship Tree was now filled with colors, shapes, and textures, each item holding a story that would live on in the garden. They felt a quiet satisfaction, knowing that they had created something beautiful and meaningful, something that would continue to grow and change as they did.

Chapter 6: The Tree's First Bloom

The children's garden around the Friendship Tree had quickly become one of their favorite places in the park. Every day after school, they would gather around their tree to talk, laugh, and check on the small plants they had added. Some days, they would sit around the tree for hours, sharing stories about their families, their dreams, and the funny things that happened in their lives. Other days, they would simply sit in silence, enjoying the peaceful space they had created together, each feeling comforted by the presence of the tree and their friends.

It was springtime now, and the garden they had planted was beginning to show signs of new life. The seeds Leo had planted from his mother's roses had started to sprout tiny green shoots, and the flowers Samira had added were beginning to open, showing flashes of color among the green. Each day, the children noticed something new—a bud here, a fresh leaf there. The garden had become a vibrant, living place, and watching it grow brought them a deep sense of pride. It felt like a symbol of all the time and care they had put into it.

One afternoon, Elara arrived at the park before anyone else. She skipped toward the Friendship Tree, her face lighting up as she spotted the familiar shape of their tree and garden in the distance. But as she got closer, she noticed something unusual. There, nestled among the leaves of their sapling, was a small bud, pale green and just beginning to show the faintest hint of color. Elara's eyes widened, and she stood still, staring at the little bud in awe. She had known their tree would bloom someday, but seeing the first bud appear filled her with a joy she hadn't expected.

Unable to contain her excitement, she ran to the tree and knelt down to look closer. The bud looked fragile but determined, as if it had pushed its way up through the branches with all its strength. It was just a small sign of life, but to Elara, it felt like a little miracle. She took out her phone and quickly sent a message to the group: "Come to the park ASAP! The Friendship Tree has a BUD!"

Within minutes, her friends arrived, each one hurrying over to the tree, their faces lighting up when they saw the small bud nestled among the leaves. They crowded around it, whispering in amazement, their excitement filling the air. For a few minutes, they simply stood there, marveling at the sight. It was only a single bud, but it felt like a victory—a sign that all their care, all the watering, all the time they had spent nurturing the tree had been worth it.

Leo, always full of ideas, suggested they celebrate the first bloom. "This is a big deal! Our tree's about to blossom for the first time. We should do something special, something to remember this moment." The others nodded eagerly, feeling the same desire to mark the occasion. After a quick discussion, they decided to hold a little ceremony that weekend. They would decorate the garden, bring snacks, and spend the afternoon celebrating the first bloom of their Friendship Tree.

Over the next few days, the children worked together to make the garden look even more beautiful. Samira painted a few new rocks with vibrant colors and designs, adding them to the edges of the garden. Leo brought a few small candles in jars, which he placed around the tree, envisioning them lighting up their celebration in the evening. Elara made little flags out of fabric and sticks, decorating them with words like "Hope," "Friendship," and "Love" before sticking them into the soil around the garden. Liam contributed a small birdhouse he had built with his dad, placing it on a low branch with the hope that a bird might someday make it its home.

When Saturday finally arrived, the children gathered in the park, their faces glowing with excitement. They had planned everything carefully, bringing blankets to sit on, snacks to share, and a small speaker to play music. As they sat together, the soft tunes floating through the air, they felt as if they were in a magical place, a place that was all their own. The sun shone warmly on their faces, and the garden around the Friendship Tree seemed to shimmer with life and color.

After a while, Leo stood up and cleared his throat, getting everyone's attention. "I just wanted to say," he began, looking around at his friends with a serious expression, "that this is the coolest thing we've ever done. I mean, we planted this tree together, and now it's blooming! That's something really special." His words were simple, but they carried the weight of all the pride and joy they felt. The others nodded in agreement, feeling the same sense of wonder at how much their tree and garden had come to mean to them.

They spent the afternoon laughing, sharing stories, and taking turns adding little items to the garden. Each addition felt like a gift to the tree, a way of saying thank you for the joy and beauty it had brought into their lives. They ate snacks, shared dreams about the future, and watched the sun slowly dip lower in the sky. As evening approached, Leo lit the candles around the garden, and they all sat together in the warm glow, feeling as though they were part of something timeless and beautiful.

As the sky darkened and the first stars began to appear, Elara turned to the group with a thoughtful look. "Do you think our tree will bloom every year?" she asked softly, gazing at the tiny bud that had brought them all together. Samira nodded, her eyes full of hope. "I think so. And I think every time it blooms, it'll remind us of today, of everything we've done together." The group fell silent, each of them imagining future springs, future blooms, and the many years they hoped to spend together around their Friendship Tree.

Eventually, it was time to head home, and the children reluctantly gathered their things, casting one last look at the tree before they left. The candles flickered gently in the breeze, casting a soft glow over the garden as if the tree itself was saying goodbye. They knew they would be back soon, but leaving felt a little harder now that they had shared such a special day with the tree. They walked home in silence, each of them carrying the memory of the day in their hearts.

The next day, they returned to the park, each of them eager to see if the little bud had bloomed. As they approached, they gasped in delight—the bud had opened, revealing a small, delicate flower with petals the color of a morning sunrise. It was a simple bloom, but it filled them with an overwhelming sense of pride and happiness. They gathered around it, admiring the soft petals, the gentle curve of the stem, and the way it seemed to reach toward the sky as if greeting the sun.

Chapter 7: Seasons of Change

As the months passed, the children continued to visit the Friendship Tree, watching it grow through the changing seasons. Their tree, once a delicate sapling, was now growing sturdier, its branches reaching a little higher each week, as if stretching to touch the sky. The garden they had planted around it thrived as well, each flower and plant transforming with the months, creating a space that reflected the rhythms of nature and time.

When summer arrived, the park became lush and full of life. The children's garden was a riot of colors, with the flowers Samira had planted blooming brightly. Leo's rose bushes had sprouted buds, and every morning, the children would rush to see if any of them had opened. The roses, when they finally bloomed, filled the garden with a soft, fragrant scent that lingered in the warm air. Butterflies flitted around the flowers, adding to the garden's magic, and the tree's leaves were a vibrant green, offering a bit of shade as they sat beneath it on the hottest days.

They spent those warm afternoons lounging under the Friendship , talking about everything and nothing, enjoying the peaceful they had created. Sometimes they would bring picnic blankets acks, sitting together in the dappled sunlight, laughing and ories. Other times, they would simply lie back and gaze up at 'eaves, which rustled softly in the breeze, their movements he laughter and friendship below. On these lazy summer ndship Tree became their shelter, a cool oasis where they e heat and enjoy each other's company.

, like all things, came to an end, and as autumn hildren noticed the first signs of change in the park. and the vibrant green leaves of the Friendship Tree or, turning a mix of gold, orange, and red. The we as their tree transformed, each new color a reminder of the beauty of change. It was the first time they had seen the tree in autumn, and they were amazed by the way the season painted its branches with fiery hues, as if it were wearing a coat of many colors.

They made it a point to visit the tree every day, eager to see how it changed from week to week. Each time they visited, the tree seemed a little different, its leaves turning deeper shades of orange and red. Sometimes they would find leaves scattered around the base of the tree, their colors bright against the cool earth. They began collecting the fallen leaves, pressing them into notebooks or bringing them home as little keepsakes of the Friendship Tree's first autumn. Every leaf, they felt, was like a memory—a reminder of the times they had spent together, of the laughter and the quiet moments shared under its branches.

As the weather grew colder, the children brought scarves and gloves, bundling up against the chill. They still gathered around the tree, though their conversations now included talk of school, of upcoming holidays, and of the plans they had for winter. They watched as the leaves began to fall in earnest, covering the ground in a soft blanket of red and gold. The tree seemed to be preparing itself for the winter, shedding its leaves in a quiet, graceful way. It was as if it were teaching them that change was a natural part of life, that letting go could be beautiful.

One day, as they sat under the nearly bare branches, Leo voiced something that had been on all their minds. "It feels kind of sad, doesn't it?" he said, looking at the scattered leaves around them. "I mean, our tree looked so full and alive just a few weeks ago. And now... it looks different." The others nodded, understanding the bittersweet feeling he was trying to express. The Friendship Tree had been so full of life in the summer, and seeing it lose its leaves made them feel as if something precious was slipping away.

Elara, always thoughtful, placed a hand on the tree's rough bark and said, "But maybe this is just a part of its journey. The tree isn't gone;

it's just changing. It's still here, and it'll come back even stronger in the spring." Her words brought comfort to the group, reminding them that change was not an end but a part of growth. They realized that just as the seasons transformed the tree, life would bring changes to their own lives, but the roots of their friendship, like the roots of the tree, would stay strong.

As winter approached, the Friendship Tree shed its last few leaves, standing bare against the gray sky. The park felt quieter now, the air sharp and cold. The children still visited the tree, but their gatherings became shorter, as the cold made it harder to stay outside for long. Even without its leaves, the Friendship Tree stood tall, its branches reaching out against the winter sky, a silent but powerful reminder of resilience.

When the first snow fell, the children rushed to the park, eager to see how their garden and the Friendship Tree would look in the winter. The garden, once full of color and life, was now blanketed in snow, the flowers and plants hidden beneath a layer of white. The tree's branches were dusted with snow, and icicles hung from the tips, sparkling in the pale winter sunlight. Though the garden and tree looked different, they were still beautiful in their own way, transformed by the season into something serene and quiet.

Bundled up in hats and scarves, the children spent an afternoon building snowmen around the tree, decorating them with sticks, rocks, and pinecones. They laughed as they made up stories for each snowman, giving them names and personalities. The Friendship Tree became the centerpiece of their winter play, its branches casting long shadows on the snow as they ran and played. Though the garden was hidden beneath the snow, they knew it was still there, waiting for the warmth of spring to bring it back to life.

As winter continued, the children learned to appreciate the stillness of the season. They visited the Friendship Tree less often, but when they did, they found comfort in its presence. Standing under its bare branches, they felt a sense of peace, as if the tree were teaching them to rest and be patient, to trust that life would bloom again in its own time. They learned to see beauty in the simplicity of winter, in the quiet strength of their tree as it stood through the cold and the snow.

Finally, after what felt like an endless winter, the first signs of spring began to appear. The snow melted, the days grew warmer, and tiny buds appeared on the branches of the Friendship Tree. The children returned to the park, overjoyed to see their tree coming back to life. They watched as the buds grew, unfurling into fresh green leaves that shimmered in the sunlight. The garden, too, began to show signs of life, with little shoots pushing up through the earth, the promise of new flowers and growth.

Seeing the Friendship Tree bloom again filled them with a sense of hope and renewal. They realized that the tree had taught them something valuable—that life was a cycle of change and growth, that each season brought its own beauty, and that they, too, would go through seasons of change. But just as the Friendship Tree endured through every season, their friendship would remain strong, growing deeper and richer with each passing year.

Chapter 8: Protecting the Tree

It was early summer when the children began to notice that something was not quite right with the Friendship Tree. They had been visiting the park regularly, enjoying the warm days and the bright colors of the garden they had planted around the tree. The flowers were in full bloom, and the leaves on the Friendship Tree were lush and green, offering a cool shade under which they could sit and chat. However, one day, as they approached the tree, Samira was the first to notice something different.

"There's a branch that looks like it's broken!" she exclaimed, her voice filled with concern. She pointed to a branch on the lower part of the tree, where a section of leaves hung limply, browning at the edges. The others gathered around, squinting up at the damaged branch. It looked out of place against the otherwise vibrant tree, as if something had harmed it. The children exchanged worried glances, each wondering what could have caused the damage.

Elara reached out to touch the injured branch gently, as though her care could somehow heal it. "Do you think it was from a storm?" she asked, glancing at the others. They considered her question, but they couldn't recall any recent storms that might have caused it. The mystery of the broken branch troubled them. They had come to see the Friendship Tree as something strong and enduring, yet here was evidence that it could still be hurt.

A few days later, as they returned to check on the tree, they discovered something even more troubling. Leo, who always arrived early, was already at the tree, standing with his arms crossed and a frown on his face. When the others reached him, they saw what had caused his frustration. Scattered around the base of the tree were bits of garbage—candy wrappers, plastic bottles, and crumpled papers, as though someone had carelessly tossed them aside.

THE FRIENDSHIP TREE

"Who would do this?" Leo muttered, his voice tinged with anger. He knelt down and began picking up the trash, grumbling under his breath. The others joined him, each of them feeling a mix of sadness and frustration. The Friendship Tree was their sanctuary, a place they had built with care, and seeing it treated so thoughtlessly felt like a personal insult. They couldn't understand why anyone would litter in a place that meant so much to them.

As they cleaned up, the children talked about how they could protect the Friendship Tree. It was clear to them that simply visiting and caring for the tree wasn't enough. They would have to make sure others understood that this tree and garden were special, not just a random spot in the park. They agreed that if they wanted the Friendship Tree to thrive, they needed to take action.

Elara suggested that they make signs asking people to keep the area clean. "If people see signs, maybe they'll think twice before throwing trash around here," she said, her eyes bright with determination. The others nodded in agreement, liking the idea. They decided to meet up later that week to create the signs, each of them excited by the thought of doing something proactive to protect their tree.

When the day arrived, they gathered at Samira's house to work on the signs. Armed with markers, paints, and blank pieces of cardboard, they got to work. They wanted the signs to be colorful and eye-catching, but also respectful and kind. Each sign bore a message that encouraged people to respect the area around the Friendship Tree. Some read, "Please Keep Our Garden Clean" or "This is a Special Place—Let's Keep It Beautiful!" Others had drawings of flowers, trees, and hearts, each one a testament to the children's love for the Friendship Tree.

As they painted, they shared ideas about other ways they could protect the tree. Leo suggested they start checking on it regularly, making sure that it stayed clean and that no more branches were damaged. Samira proposed that they talk to some of the regular visitors in the park, telling them about the Friendship Tree and why it was important. The idea made them a little nervous, but they agreed that it might make a difference. If people knew the story of the Friendship Tree, maybe they would feel more connected to it and would want to take care of it too.

The next day, the children proudly carried their signs to the park, each of them holding one of the creations they had made. They carefully placed them around the garden, making sure they were visible but not too intrusive. They stepped back to admire their work, feeling a sense of accomplishment and pride. Their signs looked cheerful and inviting, like little reminders of the love and care they had poured into the Friendship Tree.

Over the next few weeks, they noticed a difference. Fewer people littered around the tree, and they didn't find any more broken branches. The signs seemed to be working, and the children felt a renewed sense of purpose. They began to see themselves as guardians of the Friendship Tree, responsible for its well-being. It was a role they took seriously, and they were proud of the impact they were making.

But one afternoon, they arrived at the park to find a new problem. As they approached the tree, they noticed a group of older kids playing nearby, their voices loud and boisterous. The children didn't think much of it until they saw one of the older kids kick one of their painted rocks, sending it skidding across the grass. The child laughed, oblivious to the damage he had done, while the others joined in, picking up rocks and tossing them around as if they were nothing more than toys.

The children's hearts sank as they watched their carefully arranged garden being disturbed. They wanted to say something, but they felt nervous and unsure. The older kids were bigger and louder, and the idea of confronting them was intimidating. However, as they saw more rocks being thrown, they knew they couldn't just stand by and watch. Elara, who usually wasn't afraid to speak her mind, took a deep breath and stepped forward, her voice trembling slightly but firm.

"Hey! Can you please stop doing that?" she called out, trying to sound braver than she felt. "This is a special garden, and we spent a lot of time making it nice. Please don't mess it up." The older kids paused, surprised to see Elara and her friends standing there, their faces serious. For a moment, it seemed as though they might argue, but something in Elara's tone made them hesitate. One of them shrugged and muttered, "Alright, whatever," before they turned and walked away, leaving the garden in peace.

As the older kids left, the children breathed a collective sigh of relief. They were proud of Elara for standing up for the Friendship Tree, but they also felt a new sense of responsibility. They realized that protecting something important sometimes meant having the courage to speak up, even when it was difficult. They gathered up the scattered rocks and carefully placed them back in their original spots, each of them feeling more connected to the garden than ever before.

From that day on, they became more vigilant. They kept an eye on the Friendship Tree, checking it regularly to make sure it remained clean and safe. They took turns visiting the park even on days when they couldn't all be together, each of them doing their part to protect the place that had become so dear to them. They spoke to other park visitors, explaining the importance of the Friendship Tree and the garden they had created around it. Little by little, more people began to show respect for the area, often stopping to admire the garden or comment on the beauty of the tree.

The children felt a deep sense of pride as they watched others come to appreciate the Friendship Tree. Their efforts were making a difference, and they saw that they had the power to influence others in positive ways. They had started as a small group of friends caring for a tree, but their dedication had grown, reaching out to the larger community. The Friendship Tree had become a symbol not only of their friendship but of the care and respect they hoped to inspire in others.

One day, they decided to make a small plaque to place at the base of the tree, explaining its significance. They wanted people to understand why the Friendship Tree was so special, why it deserved to be treated with care. The plaque read, "The Friendship Tree: Planted with love and care by friends who believe in kindness, respect, and the power of growing together. Please help us keep this place special." It was a simple message, but one that captured everything they felt.

As they stood around the tree, reading the plaque they had made, they felt a deep sense of satisfaction. They knew that they had not only protected the Friendship Tree but had also grown in ways they hadn't expected. They had become caretakers, guardians of a place that held their dreams and memories. And in doing so, they had strengthened their own bonds, learning that friendship was about more than just sharing good times; it was about standing up for each other, for the things they cared about, and for the values they believed in.

Chapter 9: The Friendship Tree Festival

Summer had returned to the park, bringing with it warm days and long, golden evenings. The Friendship Tree stood proudly in the middle of its garden, surrounded by the blooming flowers and the little keepsakes the children had added over the seasons. The area had become a vibrant, living space, filled with colors, scents, and memories. People who walked by often stopped to admire it, smiling as they read the sign that the children had placed by the tree months before. The Friendship Tree had become a beloved part of the park, a place where people gathered, relaxed, and appreciated the beauty of nature.

As the summer days rolled on, the children found themselves spending more and more time at the tree, their conversations often wandering to all the things they had done together. They laughed about the time they had first planted it, reminisced about decorating the garden, and remembered how they had protected the tree from careless visitors. But as they talked, they all began to feel that they wanted to do something special to celebrate their friendship and everything the tree had come to mean to them. After all, the Friendship Tree was more than just a tree now—it was a symbol of everything they shared and believed in.

It was Samira who first voiced the idea. "What if we threw a festival? Like a Friendship Tree Festival?" she said, her eyes sparkling with excitement. "We could invite our families, our friends, and everyone from the neighborhood. It could be a way to show everyone what the tree means to us." The others looked at her with wide eyes, letting the idea sink in. A festival sounded like a wonderful way to celebrate not only the Friendship Tree but also the friendships that had grown around it.

Leo was the first to respond, his face lighting up with enthusiasm. "That's an amazing idea! We could decorate the whole area, have games, maybe even bring some food. It could be a whole day of celebrating."

The others nodded eagerly, their minds already spinning with ideas. They imagined a day filled with laughter, music, and activities, a day where everyone could come together to enjoy the space they had created. It would be a way to share the joy of the Friendship Tree with others, to make new memories and connections.

They spent the next few days planning every detail, each of them contributing ideas for the festival. Elara suggested they make invitations, colorful cards that they could hand out at school and around the neighborhood. Samira offered to paint a big banner that would hang from the tree, welcoming everyone to the Friendship Tree Festival. Leo thought about the games they could play, imagining activities that both kids and adults could enjoy. And Liam, who was always thoughtful, suggested that they create a small area where people could leave messages or notes about what friendship meant to them.

As they worked on their plans, they realized that organizing a festival would be a big task. There were decorations to prepare, food to arrange, games to plan, and countless other details to consider. But instead of feeling overwhelmed, they felt excited, energized by the idea of creating something meaningful. They decided to ask their families for help, knowing that their parents and siblings would be happy to support them.

When they shared their idea with their families, they were met with smiles and enthusiasm. Their parents loved the thought of a Friendship Tree Festival, not only because it was a celebration but also because it was a way for the children to share the story of the Friendship Tree with the community. Their parents offered to help with food and decorations, and their siblings jumped at the chance to join in, each one contributing in their own way. With the support of their families, the children felt even more motivated, knowing they were working together toward something special.

The days leading up to the festival were filled with preparation. Samira spent hours painting the banner, carefully lettering "Welcome to the Friendship Tree Festival" in bold, bright colors. Leo and Elara designed a set of games, including a relay race, a treasure hunt, and a "Friendship Tag" game where people had to pair up to complete challenges together. Liam set up the message area, decorating a small table with flowers and paper for people to write notes. Each detail was planned with care, and every moment they spent preparing felt like another layer added to their friendship.

Finally, the day of the festival arrived, and the park was filled with a lively buzz of excitement. The children arrived early in the morning, carrying supplies and decorations. Together, they hung up the banner, set up tables, and arranged the games. By the time everything was ready, the area around the Friendship Tree looked like a little festival ground, filled with color and activity. The tree itself stood tall and proud in the middle of it all, as if it, too, were ready to join in the celebration.

People began arriving in the early afternoon, families and friends from around the neighborhood drawn by the bright decorations and the joyful atmosphere. The children greeted each guest, explaining the story of the Friendship Tree to those who didn't know it. They told of how they had planted it together, how they had protected and cared for it, and how it had grown into something much larger than they had ever imagined. As people listened, they looked at the tree with new appreciation, understanding that it was more than just a part of the park—it was a symbol of friendship, unity, and love.

The games and activities were a hit with both kids and adults. Families laughed as they participated in the relay race, while children eagerly joined the treasure hunt, searching for small prizes hidden around the garden. The message table became a popular spot, with people stopping by to write notes about friendship and to leave small tokens or keepsakes for the Friendship Tree. Some left drawings, others wrote poems, and a few even shared stories about their own friends and loved ones. By the end of the day, the table was covered with messages, each one a reminder of the connections that bound them all together.

As the festival went on, laughter and music filled the air, creating an atmosphere of warmth and joy. The children moved around, greeting friends, sharing stories, and watching as people joined in the celebration. They felt a deep sense of happiness and pride, knowing that they had created something that brought people together. The festival wasn't just a celebration of the tree—it was a celebration of community, of the bonds that connected each person to the other.

Chapter 10: A Lesson in Patience

It had been a few weeks since the Friendship Tree Festival, and the children still talked about it with excitement every time they gathered around their tree. The memory of the festival filled them with pride and a sense of accomplishment; they felt like they had created something truly magical for their community. They still spent most of their afternoons in the park, sharing stories and adding small touches to their garden whenever they thought of new ideas. They watched as the roses bloomed, the leaves rustled in the warm breeze, and the days slowly grew shorter, signaling the approach of autumn once again.

As the new season approached, the children began to talk more about their hopes for the future. They imagined how tall the Friendship Tree would grow, picturing it reaching up into the sky, with branches thick and strong enough to provide shade to generations of park visitors. They envisioned how the tree would look in five years, in ten years, and even dreamed about how it might be someday, tall and majestic, a permanent fixture in the park. They felt a deep sense of attachment to the tree, and with it came a desire to see it grow faster, to become the towering symbol of friendship they had imagined.

One afternoon, as they sat around the tree discussing their dreams, Leo voiced what they had all been thinking. "I just wish it would grow faster," he said, frowning slightly as he looked up at the young tree. "I mean, look at it—it's grown a little since we planted it, but it's still so small." The others nodded, sharing his frustration. They had poured so much of their love and care into the tree, and though it had grown since they first planted it, it still didn't look like the towering tree they had imagined.

Elara, always full of ideas, suggested that they try something to help the tree grow faster. "Maybe we could give it more water or find some kind of plant food that would make it grow quicker," she said eagerly. "There has to be something we can do to help it along." The others agreed, excited by the idea of speeding up the tree's growth. They decided to look for ways to give their tree an extra boost, hoping it would bring them closer to the future they dreamed of.

Over the next few days, they each brought things they thought might help. Leo's dad, who loved gardening, suggested adding a little extra compost around the base of the tree, so Leo brought a small bag from home and sprinkled it around the roots. Samira's mom offered some plant food, explaining that it could provide nutrients to the tree. Samira carefully mixed the plant food with water, pouring it around the base of the tree and making sure not to spill too much. Elara even read up on how trees grow, sharing tips she found online with the group. She suggested that they talk to the tree, as she had read that plants responded well to kindness and attention. They each took turns talking to the tree, whispering encouragements and telling it about the future they saw for it.

For weeks, the children tried everything they could think of. They watered it more frequently, checked the soil daily, and even removed any weeds that grew nearby. They monitored every new leaf and every inch of growth, hoping to see a sudden change. But despite all their efforts, the Friendship Tree remained the same. It was healthy and green, its leaves rustling in the wind, but it did not grow any faster. The children felt a mixture of disappointment and confusion. They had put in so much effort, yet their tree was still small, growing at its own natural pace.

One day, as they gathered around the tree, Leo let out a sigh of frustration. "I don't get it. We've done everything we can, but it's still so slow. Why won't it just grow?" His voice carried a note of impatience that the others understood all too well. They all felt the same way. The more they tried to speed up the process, the more they realized that some things were simply beyond their control.

Liam, who was usually quiet but thoughtful, spoke up after a moment. "Maybe... maybe the tree doesn't need us to rush it," he said, choosing his words carefully. "Maybe it's just going to grow at its own pace, no matter what we do." The others looked at him, considering his words. They knew he was right. Trees didn't grow overnight, and no amount of extra water or plant food could change that. It was a hard lesson, but they could see the truth in it.

As they sat in silence, reflecting on Liam's words, an elderly woman who had been watching them from a nearby bench approached. She had seen them around the tree often, watering it, talking to it, and taking care of it with a devotion that touched her heart. Smiling, she asked if she could join them, and the children nodded, curious to hear what she had to say.

She settled down on the grass beside them, her eyes warm and wise. "I couldn't help but notice how much you all care for this tree," she began, glancing up at its slender branches. "It's a beautiful thing, to care for something that you hope will grow and flourish. But have you ever thought about why trees grow slowly?"

The children looked at each other, unsure of what she meant. Leo shrugged. "We just wanted it to grow faster so we could see it big and strong," he admitted, his tone a mix of longing and frustration.

The woman nodded, understanding their impatience. "I felt the same way when I planted a tree with my friends many years ago," she said, her voice filled with nostalgia. "But what I learned is that the strength of a tree doesn't come from how quickly it grows. It comes from its roots, from the time it spends reaching deep into the soil, finding its foundation. The slower it grows, the stronger it becomes."

Her words resonated with the children, each of them feeling a newfound respect for the tree's slow, steady growth. She continued, "Trees teach us patience. They teach us to trust in the process, to know that everything will happen in its own time. You're already doing everything you can for this tree, and that's all it needs. It will grow, just as you will, and someday it will be as tall and strong as you've imagined. But only if you give it the time it needs."

The children thanked the woman, her wisdom settling over them like a warm blanket. They realized that in their eagerness to see the tree grow, they had forgotten to appreciate its journey, to trust that it would become everything they hoped for, in its own time. The woman left, and they stayed under the tree for a while, feeling a sense of calm they hadn't felt before. They looked at the Friendship Tree with new eyes, seeing its steady growth as a reminder that everything valuable in life takes time to develop.

Chapter 11: Roots Run Deep

It was a chilly autumn morning when the children noticed something new about their Friendship Tree. The vibrant colors of summer had faded, and now the park was dressed in shades of red, orange, and yellow. The ground was covered with fallen leaves, and the air had a crispness that made them pull their scarves a little tighter. They gathered around the tree as they did every morning, admiring the way it had transformed with the season. Although the Friendship Tree had shed most of its leaves, there was a certain beauty in its bare branches. The tree seemed to stand tall and proud, its branches stretching out against the clear blue sky.

As they sat together, Samira noticed something unusual near the base of the tree. She knelt down and pointed at a spot on the ground where the roots of the tree were visible, pushing slightly through the soil. "Look at that!" she exclaimed, her voice filled with wonder. "It's like we can see its roots." The others gathered around, each of them gazing at the exposed roots in awe. They had never thought much about the roots before; to them, the tree had always been about the leaves, the branches, and the flowers. But now, seeing the roots just below the surface, they realized that there was so much more to their Friendship Tree than what they could see above the ground.

Leo, who was always curious, reached out and gently touched one of the roots. "These roots are holding up the whole tree," he said thoughtfully. "They're hidden most of the time, but they're what's keeping the tree strong." The children looked at each other, each of them sensing the importance of what Leo had just said. They had spent so much time caring for the branches, the leaves, and the flowers, but now they realized that the roots—the part of the tree they couldn't see—were just as vital.

Elara, who had always loved learning about nature, explained, "The roots are like the tree's anchor. They go deep into the ground to find water and nutrients, and they keep the tree steady when there's a storm." The children listened, fascinated by this new understanding of their tree. They began to see that the roots were more than just part of the tree; they were the foundation, the part that allowed everything else to grow. Without strong roots, the tree couldn't survive.

As they sat in silence, reflecting on what they had learned, they began to think about their own lives and friendships. Samira, always insightful, spoke up. "Maybe our friendship is like the roots of the tree," she said quietly. "I mean, we can't always see everything that keeps us connected, but it's there, holding us together." Her words struck a chord with the group, and they each thought about the moments that had built their friendship, the unspoken understanding and trust that had grown between them over time.

Inspired by their discovery, they decided to dig a little around the base of the tree to learn more about its roots. They were careful not to harm anything, but as they uncovered more of the roots, they were amazed by what they saw. The roots spread out in all directions, twisting and turning through the soil, reaching deeper and farther than they had imagined. Some roots were thin and delicate, while others were thick and sturdy, like the tree's support beams. Each root was connected to the others, creating a complex network that held the tree firmly in place.

As they studied the roots, they noticed how they intertwined with one another, forming a web of support. It reminded them of the ways their own lives were connected. Each of them came from different families, had different interests, and dreamed of different futures, yet they were all part of the same network, just like the roots of the tree. They realized that their friendship had many layers, some of which they didn't even think about, but that were essential to keeping them close.

Over the next few days, they found themselves talking more about the roots and what they symbolized. They thought about the quiet ways they supported each other, the small acts of kindness and understanding that strengthened their friendship. They realized that their bond wasn't just about the fun moments they shared; it was also about being there for each other, even when things weren't easy. It was the quiet, unseen moments that made their friendship strong, just like the roots made the tree strong.

One evening, after a particularly windy day, they returned to the park to check on the Friendship Tree. The wind had scattered leaves everywhere, and some of the smaller plants around the garden had been knocked over. The tree itself, however, stood tall and unharmed, its roots holding it firmly in place. The sight of the tree standing strong after the storm filled them with pride and admiration. They had been worried that the tree might have been damaged, but now they understood just how resilient it was.

As they stood around the tree, Leo remarked, "I think we're kind of like this tree. When things get tough, we help each other stay strong." The others nodded, each of them thinking about times when their friends had helped them through difficult moments. They realized that their friendship, like the tree's roots, provided a foundation that helped them stand tall even when life was challenging. It was a comforting thought, knowing that they had each other's support no matter what.

They decided to write notes to each other, expressing what their friendship meant to them. They gathered small pieces of paper and wrote messages of gratitude and appreciation, words that they had never spoken aloud but had always felt. Each note was like a little piece of the roots, a reminder of the strength and love that held them together. They placed the notes in a small box and buried it near the roots of the tree, a symbol of their commitment to one another and the unseen support that made their friendship strong.

As they placed the box in the ground, they each made a silent promise to be there for one another, just as the roots were there for the tree. They knew that there would be challenges ahead, but they felt prepared to face them together. They understood now that their friendship wasn't just about the fun times or the laughter; it was about the deeper connection they shared, the invisible roots that held them close even when they couldn't see them.

The experience of discovering the roots changed the way they looked at their friendship and at life. They began to notice the quiet moments that connected them, the small acts of kindness, the unspoken understanding. They appreciated the roots of their friendship—the moments of patience, support, and love that kept them strong. And as they looked at the Friendship Tree, they knew that it would continue to grow, supported by the roots that ran deep beneath the ground, just as their friendship would continue to flourish, supported by the bond they shared.

In the weeks that followed, they found themselves paying more attention to the roots of their friendship, the small but meaningful gestures that strengthened their bond. They celebrated each other's successes, comforted each other in difficult times, and offered support whenever it was needed. They realized that friendship was about more than just shared interests and fun moments; it was about being there for each other in ways that weren't always visible, but were always felt.

Chapter 12: A Year in Reflection

As winter approached and the year drew to a close, the children found themselves spending less time at the park. The days grew shorter, the air became colder, and soon, the first snow covered the ground around the Friendship Tree. The park looked different in winter, serene and quiet, with its usual colors softened by a blanket of white. The Friendship Tree stood bare, its branches reaching toward the gray sky, and the garden they had so carefully tended was hidden beneath a layer of snow. Despite the chill in the air, the children made a point of visiting the tree from time to time, bundled up in coats and scarves, their breath puffing in clouds as they laughed and talked together.

One afternoon, as they gathered around the tree, they decided to reflect on the past year, talking about everything they had shared and experienced together. They each felt a sense of pride and accomplishment as they recalled how the Friendship Tree had started as a small sapling, a simple idea that had grown into something much larger than they had ever imagined. It had become a part of them, a living testament to their bond, and looking back over the year, they realized just how much it had shaped their friendship.

Leo, who often spoke first, broke the silence. "It's hard to believe we planted this tree almost a year ago," he said, looking up at the branches with a thoughtful expression. "Remember how we all brought soil from our homes? I can still picture us mixing it together, making sure every piece was part of it." The others nodded, smiling as they remembered that first day. It had been the beginning of something they could never have predicted, and thinking back to that moment filled them with a deep sense of nostalgia.

Samira added, "And look at everything we've done since then! We made a garden, we decorated it, and we even held a festival for the whole neighborhood." Her voice was filled with pride, and the others echoed her sentiment. Each of them remembered the joy and excitement of creating the garden, of adding their own special touches, and of seeing people from the community come together for the festival. It was a memory that brought warmth to their hearts, even on the coldest days.

Elara, who often saw things from a broader perspective, spoke up next. "I think what I love most is that the tree has changed us, too. We've learned so much from it, more than I ever thought we would." Her words made the others pause, each of them reflecting on the lessons they had learned over the past year. They thought about the patience they had developed, the understanding they had gained, and the quiet ways the Friendship Tree had taught them about growth, resilience, and kindness.

As they continued to share memories, they realized that each of them had taken something different from their time with the tree. For Leo, it was a lesson in responsibility; he had taken pride in caring for the tree, in making sure it had water and that the garden was free of litter. For Samira, it was about creativity and expression; she loved how the garden had become a canvas for her art, a place where she could share her colorful ideas with her friends and the world. Elara felt that the tree had taught her about patience, about trusting in the process and understanding that growth took time. And for Liam, the tree represented strength and stability; it was a reminder that even in times of change, there were things he could count on.

They decided to do something special to mark the end of the year, to honor the journey they had taken together. Elara suggested they write letters to their future selves, describing everything they had learned from the Friendship Tree and their hopes for the future. Each of them would write a letter and seal it in an envelope, and they would place the letters in a small box, burying it near the roots of the tree as a time capsule of sorts. The idea filled them with excitement, and they agreed to meet again on the weekend to write their letters together.

When the weekend arrived, they gathered at Elara's house, where her parents had set up a cozy spot by the fireplace for them. The room was warm and inviting, with blankets and hot chocolate to keep them comfortable as they settled in to write. Each of them held a blank piece of paper, their minds filled with memories and thoughts about what they wanted to say. The idea of writing to their future selves felt a little strange, but also exciting, as though they were sending a message across time.

Leo was the first to put pen to paper. He wrote about the pride he felt in taking care of the tree, about how it had shown him the importance of responsibility and dedication. He wrote about the small acts, like picking up litter and watering the garden, that had taught him that taking care of something was a way of showing love. He ended his letter with a promise to always care for the things he valued, to be mindful of his actions and their impact.

Samira's letter was filled with color and imagination. She drew little doodles in the margins and wrote about the joy she had found in adding her own touch to the garden, about how the Friendship Tree had given her a place to express herself. She wrote about the festival and the happiness it had brought to everyone who attended, and how sharing her art with others had filled her with a sense of purpose. She promised herself to always find ways to create and to share that joy with others.

Elara's letter was reflective, full of quiet wisdom. She wrote about the patience the tree had taught her, about how it had shown her that growth couldn't be rushed and that everything happened in its own time. She thought about the times they had tried to make the tree grow faster, and how she had learned to appreciate each step in its journey. She ended her letter with a reminder to herself to be patient, to trust in the process, and to enjoy each moment as it came.

Liam's letter was simple but heartfelt. He wrote about the strength he had found in the Friendship Tree, about how it had become a symbol of stability for him. He described how he had come to see the tree as a friend, a constant presence that he could rely on, and how that feeling of stability had made him feel more secure. He ended his letter with a promise to be strong and steady, like the tree, for his friends and family.

When they had finished writing, they placed their letters in envelopes, sealing each one carefully. They decorated the envelopes with little drawings and stickers, each of them adding a personal touch to their letter. Finally, they placed the letters in a small wooden box that Elara's dad had given them, a box that was just the right size to hold their hopes, dreams, and memories.

The next day, they took the box to the park, their breath fogging in the cold air as they walked to the Friendship Tree. The ground was hard with frost, but they managed to dig a small hole near the base of the tree. They placed the box in the ground, each of them taking a moment to reflect on what it represented. It was more than just a collection of letters; it was a promise to themselves and to each other, a commitment to carry forward the lessons they had learned from the tree.

As they covered the box with soil, they felt a sense of closure, as though they were wrapping up one chapter of their lives and preparing for the next. They knew that the tree would continue to grow, that the garden would bloom again in spring, and that they would always have this place to remind them of who they were and what they had learned. They stood in silence for a moment, feeling the weight of their commitment and the strength of their bond.

Over the next few days, the park grew even quieter as winter set in. The children visited the Friendship Tree less often, their lives busy with school and family commitments. But every time they walked by the park, they felt a surge of warmth, knowing that the tree was there, standing tall and strong, with their memories and promises buried safely at its roots.

As the months passed and the year came to a close, they found themselves looking forward to the future with a sense of hope and excitement. They didn't know what the coming year would bring, but they knew that they would face it together, supported by the lessons they had learned from the Friendship Tree. They felt ready for whatever lay ahead, confident that their friendship and the tree's quiet strength would guide them through the challenges and joys of life.

Chapter 13: Adapting to Challenges

The winter months settled over the park like a thick, quiet blanket, transforming the familiar landscape into something almost magical. Snow dusted the ground, clung to the branches of the Friendship Tree, and softened every edge in sight. The children visited the park less often now, braving the cold only occasionally to check on their tree, now standing bare but resilient in the chilly air. It was a peaceful time for the Friendship Tree, a season of rest and quiet strength, and although the children missed gathering around it, they knew the tree was patiently waiting for spring.

Then, one blustery morning in early March, a powerful windstorm swept through their town. It was fierce and relentless, howling through the streets and tearing through the park with a force that the children had never seen before. They watched from their windows as trees bent and swayed, their branches thrashing against the wind. The storm lasted for hours, and as the children listened to the howling wind, they couldn't help but worry about the Friendship Tree. Would it withstand the storm? Would their garden survive? They all felt a mix of anxiety and helplessness, knowing there was nothing they could do but wait.

The next morning, as soon as the sun peeked over the horizon, they hurried to the park, hoping for the best but fearing the worst. As they approached, their hearts sank. The once familiar landscape looked different, scattered with fallen branches and debris. Trees that had stood for years had lost limbs, some uprooted entirely. It was a strange and unsettling sight, and the children felt a pang of sadness as they moved through the park, taking in the storm's impact.

When they reached the Friendship Tree, they stopped, their hearts pounding. The tree was still standing, but it looked battered and weary. One of its larger branches had been broken, hanging limply by a few fibers of bark. Some of the smaller branches were bent or twisted, and the garden around it was littered with leaves, broken twigs, and uprooted plants. Their beloved Friendship Tree, which had weathered so many seasons and so much care, now looked fragile and wounded. The sight was heartbreaking, and for a moment, they just stood there, not sure what to do.

Leo was the first to speak, his voice quiet but filled with determination. "We have to help it," he said, looking around at the others. "We can't just leave it like this." His words sparked something in the group, and they all nodded, their sadness turning into a fierce resolve. This tree, which had come to mean so much to them, needed their help now more than ever. They didn't know exactly how to fix it, but they were willing to try, to do whatever they could to restore the Friendship Tree and their garden.

They spent the morning carefully clearing the debris around the tree, picking up broken branches and leaves and gently placing them to the side. Elara took out a small pair of gardening shears she had borrowed from her mom and used them to trim the broken branch, carefully cutting away the damaged parts. She worked with a steady hand, her face set with concentration. Leo and Liam helped her, holding the branch steady and making sure she didn't miss any of the splintered wood. They all moved with care, as if tending to an injured friend.

Samira, meanwhile, focused on the garden. Many of the flowers and plants they had carefully tended over the past year were damaged or uprooted, their stems bent and their petals torn. She gently replanted the flowers, pressing the soil around them and whispering encouragement, as if her words alone could bring them back to life. As she worked, she felt a deep connection to the plants and the earth, a sense of responsibility that went beyond simple care. This garden was part of her, part of all of them, and she wanted to make sure it would bloom again.

The children worked for hours, their hands cold and their faces pink from the chilly air, but they didn't stop. They took breaks only when they needed to warm up, huddling together and sharing snacks they had brought. Despite the hard work, there was a sense of quiet joy in the air, a feeling that they were doing something meaningful, something that truly mattered. They weren't just cleaning up a garden; they were restoring something they loved, something that had given them so much joy and strength.

As the day wore on, they began to realize that their efforts would not be enough to fully restore the tree and garden on their own. They would need more help, more knowledge, and possibly even more tools. But rather than feeling defeated, they saw it as a new challenge, a chance to learn and grow. They decided to seek advice from a local gardener who often worked in the park. They had seen her tending to the flower beds and shrubs, and they knew she would have the expertise they needed.

The next day, they found the gardener, a kind woman named Ms. Hensley, and explained their situation. She listened patiently, nodding as they described the damage and their efforts to repair it. She agreed to help, her eyes soft with admiration as she saw the dedication and love the children had for their tree. She offered to teach them a few techniques to help the tree recover and even provided some tools they could borrow.

Under Ms. Hensley's guidance, the children learned about pruning, soil health, and how to support a damaged tree. She showed them how to cut away dead wood to prevent disease, how to check for pests that could harm the tree, and how to use stakes to support weak branches. They listened intently, absorbing every piece of advice, eager to apply what they learned. They returned to the tree with renewed determination, armed with new skills and knowledge.

The experience of restoring the Friendship Tree brought the children closer than ever before. They learned to work as a team, each of them taking on different responsibilities, sharing their strengths, and supporting each other through the challenging days. They found a rhythm in their work, an understanding that each small task, no matter how minor, contributed to the larger goal. And in those moments of quiet focus, as they worked side by side, they felt a deep sense of peace and purpose.

One chilly evening, after they had finished their work for the day, they sat under the tree, admiring the progress they had made. The Friendship Tree looked stronger, its branches stretching out once more, and the garden was beginning to resemble its former beauty. They felt a mixture of pride and relief, knowing that their hard work was paying off. They had faced a challenge, one that had initially seemed overwhelming, and they had met it with resilience, creativity, and love.

Elara, who had grown thoughtful during their work, broke the silence. "You know," she said, "I think this has shown us that things don't always stay perfect. Sometimes, even things we love go through hard times, but that doesn't mean they're broken forever." Her words resonated with the others, each of them reflecting on the ways their friendship had been tested and strengthened through the experience.

Chapter 14: Celebrating Differences

With the return of spring, the park bloomed back to life, filling with the sights and sounds that had faded during the quiet months of winter. The Friendship Tree, which had withstood the fierce winter storms, stood proudly once again, its branches covered in fresh green leaves. The garden around it flourished with vibrant colors, a living testament to the hard work and love the children had poured into it. They felt an immense sense of pride as they watched the tree grow stronger and more beautiful with each passing day.

One sunny afternoon, the children gathered under the Friendship Tree, each bringing something small from their homes to add to the garden. They wanted to add new items to reflect their growth and to celebrate the way their friendship had evolved over the past year. As they sat together, sharing their stories and ideas, Elara spoke up with a thoughtful expression. "Do you know what I love about us?" she asked, glancing around at her friends. "We're all so different. We each bring something unique to this friendship."

The others nodded, reflecting on Elara's words. They had often noticed how different they all were, how each of them approached life in their own unique way. Samira loved colors, painting, and creativity; Leo was adventurous, always ready for a new challenge; Elara was thoughtful and reflective, often seeing things from a broader perspective; and Liam, though quieter than the others, brought a calm wisdom and gentle strength to the group. Their differences had sometimes led to misunderstandings, but they had come to realize that these differences were what made their friendship so special.

Samira, with her usual enthusiasm, suggested that they each take a turn sharing something that made them different, something that defined who they were. She explained that by talking about their unique qualities, they could learn more about each other and appreciate the individual strengths they each brought to their friendship. The others agreed, intrigued by the idea of exploring their differences in a positive way.

Samira volunteered to go first, her eyes shining with excitement. She talked about her love for art, describing how colors and shapes filled her mind whenever she saw something beautiful. She explained how painting allowed her to express emotions and ideas that were sometimes hard to put into words. As she spoke, the others listened intently, gaining a new appreciation for the way Samira saw the world. They had always admired her art, but hearing her talk about it in her own words helped them understand how deeply her creativity was woven into who she was.

When Samira finished, Leo spoke up, a grin on his face. He shared how much he loved exploring and trying new things, whether it was climbing trees, riding his bike through the forest, or even learning new games. He explained that his curiosity often got him into trouble, but that he wouldn't change it for anything. Exploring made him feel alive, like every day was an adventure waiting to happen. His friends laughed, recognizing the truth in his words. They had all been on the receiving end of Leo's boundless energy, but they appreciated how his adventurous spirit had brought a sense of excitement and discovery to their friendship.

Next, it was Elara's turn. She spoke slowly, choosing her words carefully as she described her love for reading, learning, and understanding things deeply. She shared how she often felt the need to think about things before acting, to make sure she was making the right choice. While her friends sometimes saw her as quiet or overly cautious, Elara explained that her thoughtful nature helped her see things in ways others might not. The others listened, nodding as they realized how much they had come to rely on Elara's insights. Her careful thinking had often helped them avoid problems, and her wisdom had brought clarity to many difficult situations.

Finally, Liam spoke, his voice soft but steady. He explained that he didn't always feel the need to talk, that he found comfort in silence and in observing the world around him. He shared how he often noticed details that others might miss, like the way the leaves on the tree moved in the breeze, or how the colors in the garden shifted with the changing light. Liam's calm presence had always been a source of comfort for the group, but hearing him describe his perspective gave them a new understanding of his quiet strength.

As they each took turns sharing, they began to see how their differences, instead of creating distance, actually brought them closer together. Each person's unique qualities filled a role in their friendship, balancing each other out and creating a harmony that they hadn't fully appreciated before. They realized that the Friendship Tree, which they had built together, was a reflection of the diversity within their group—a blend of different perspectives, strengths, and dreams, all growing together in the same place.

After everyone had shared, they fell into a comfortable silence, each of them lost in their own thoughts. Samira broke the silence with an idea. "Why don't we create something together that shows how different we all are, but how we still belong together?" she suggested, her face lighting up with inspiration. "We could each make something to represent ourselves, and then place it around the Friendship Tree as a symbol of our friendship."

The others loved the idea, and they agreed to spend the next week working on their individual projects. They each thought carefully about what they wanted to create, something that would capture their essence and represent their unique contribution to the group. The thought of creating something personal and then sharing it with their friends felt exciting and meaningful, a way to celebrate their individuality within the friendship they cherished.

Over the next few days, they each worked on their projects, pouring their hearts and creativity into their creations. When the week was up, they gathered at the Friendship Tree, eager to see what each person had made.

Samira was the first to reveal her project. She had painted a small wooden rock with swirling colors, each layer representing a different emotion or memory. The colors blended together in a vibrant, mesmerizing pattern that captured her love for art and self-expression. She explained how each color held a special meaning, reflecting her joy, her dreams, and her hopes for the future. Her friends admired the beauty of her creation, feeling the warmth and energy she had poured into every brushstroke.

Leo went next, proudly presenting a small, handmade compass he had fashioned from an old piece of metal. He explained how the compass represented his adventurous spirit, his desire to explore and discover new things. Although it didn't actually point north, he said with a grin, it reminded him to always follow his curiosity, to stay true to himself no matter where life took him. His friends laughed, appreciating the cleverness of his creation and the sense of adventure that had become such an essential part of their friendship.

Chapter 15: Facing Difficult Choices

As spring continued to unfold, the park blossomed into a lush and vibrant space once more. The children's beloved Friendship Tree grew greener by the day, and the garden around it flourished with color and life. The children visited the tree regularly, basking in the warmth of the season, and sharing stories, dreams, and laughter. But one day, a surprise awaited them that would test their friendship in ways they hadn't anticipated.

It began as a normal afternoon. They had all gathered around the tree, discussing plans for the summer and excitedly talking about the things they wanted to do together. Just as Leo was describing a new trail he wanted to explore, an older man approached them, accompanied by a few other adults. He introduced himself as Mr. Calloway, a member of the town council, and explained that he was leading a project to improve the park. The children were initially thrilled—more activities, better playgrounds, and even a picnic area were all part of the plans he described. But as he continued, they noticed his expression change slightly.

Mr. Calloway took a deep breath and said, "One of the things we're planning is a new walking path that will go right through this area. It's part of a larger plan to make the park more accessible." The children's smiles began to fade as they sensed something troubling in his tone. He continued, "Unfortunately, this means we'll need to clear some space, including this part of the park. The Friendship Tree would have to be removed to make way for the path."

For a moment, the world seemed to stop. The children looked at each other, their hearts sinking as the reality of his words hit them. The Friendship Tree, their tree, the place that had become a symbol of their friendship, was at risk of being cut down. It was almost too much to process, and each of them felt a knot of worry and sadness growing in their stomachs. They had spent so much time and love caring for the tree, creating memories around it, and now the thought of losing it felt unbearable.

Seeing their distress, Mr. Calloway tried to reassure them. "I know this is hard to hear," he said gently, "but the path will benefit the whole community, and it's a decision the town council made after a lot of thought. We'll make sure to plant another tree in another part of the park, and I promise we'll make it special." But his words did little to comfort them. The children could only stare at the Friendship Tree, each of them feeling a deep sadness at the thought of losing it.

After Mr. Calloway and his team left, the children sat in silence, grappling with their emotions. They had faced challenges before, but this felt different. This was something beyond their control, something they couldn't fix with hard work or patience. They spent a long time sitting together, each of them lost in their thoughts, until Elara finally spoke up. "We have to do something," she said, her voice quiet but determined. "We can't just let them take our tree away."

The others nodded, sharing her determination. They knew they had to try, even if it seemed impossible. They began brainstorming ideas, coming up with plans to protect the Friendship Tree. Leo suggested they write a petition, gathering signatures from people in the community who also valued the tree and wanted it to stay. Samira proposed creating posters to spread the word, explaining the significance of the Friendship Tree and why it was important to them. Liam, who was always calm and practical, suggested they talk to other members of the town council to see if there was a way to change their minds.

They spent the next week working tirelessly on their campaign. They made posters with bright colors and bold letters, each one expressing their love for the Friendship Tree and asking others to support their cause. They spoke to people in the park, sharing stories about the tree and what it meant to them, explaining how it had become a part of their lives and their friendship. Their energy and passion were contagious, and soon, others in the community began to rally behind them. People signed their petition, offering words of encouragement and support, and some even shared their own stories about how the tree had been a meaningful part of their visits to the park.

As the days passed, the children grew more hopeful. They saw the community coming together, united by a shared appreciation for the Friendship Tree. They felt that maybe, just maybe, their efforts would be enough to change the town council's decision. The thought of saving the tree filled them with pride and optimism, and they felt closer than ever, working together toward a common goal.

Finally, the day arrived when they were scheduled to meet with the town council. They dressed in their best clothes, each of them carrying a sense of purpose and determination. They stood before the council, presenting their petition and explaining their reasons for wanting to save the tree. They spoke with honesty and emotion, describing the memories they had made around the tree and the lessons it had taught them. Elara read a heartfelt letter she had written, explaining how the Friendship Tree had become a symbol of unity and growth, not just for them but for the entire community.

When they finished, the council members sat in thoughtful silence. Mr. Calloway, who was present, looked at them with sympathy but remained quiet, waiting for the council to deliberate. After what felt like an eternity, the council's chairperson spoke, her voice kind but firm. She praised the children's dedication and acknowledged the importance of the tree to their friendship. However, she explained that the decision to build the path had already been finalized, and that changing the plan at this stage would be extremely difficult.

The children felt a wave of disappointment wash over them. Despite all their efforts, it seemed that the Friendship Tree's fate was already sealed. They left the meeting in silence, each of them feeling a heavy sadness as they realized that they might lose the tree they loved so much. They walked back to the park together, their hearts heavy, and sat under the Friendship Tree, feeling a sense of loss that words couldn't fully capture.

For a while, they simply sat together, letting the silence speak for them. Then, Leo, who was usually full of energy, spoke in a quiet voice. "Maybe this is part of the tree's journey, just like we have our own journeys," he said, his gaze fixed on the tree's branches swaying gently in the breeze. His words brought a sense of acceptance to the group, a reminder that sometimes, things were beyond their control. They realized that while they might not be able to change the town council's decision, they could still honor the Friendship Tree in their own way.

Over the next few days, they talked about ways to preserve the memory of the Friendship Tree, even if it couldn't remain standing. Samira suggested they each take a small piece of the garden home, like a flower or a handful of soil, as a keepsake. Elara proposed that they create a scrapbook filled with photos, drawings, and notes about the tree, something they could look back on whenever they wanted to remember the special times they had shared.

As they worked on their project, they found that the act of remembering brought them comfort. They gathered photos they had taken over the past year, each one capturing a moment of joy, growth, or reflection around the Friendship Tree. They wrote letters to the tree, expressing their gratitude for everything it had taught them, and included stories and memories that held a special place in their hearts. They filled the scrapbook with drawings, pressed flowers, and small tokens from the garden, creating a beautiful tribute to the tree and the role it had played in their lives.

On the day the construction was scheduled to begin, they gathered at the park one last time. They sat together under the tree, each holding a small piece of the garden they had taken as a keepsake. They didn't say much, letting the silence speak for the emotions they couldn't put into words. They knew this would be their final moment with the

Friendship Tree, but instead of feeling sadness, they felt a deep sense of peace. They had done everything they could to protect it, and while they hadn't succeeded in the way they had hoped, they knew they had honored the tree's memory in their own way.

Chapter 16: Planting New Seeds

As the weeks passed after saying goodbye to the Friendship Tree, life gradually returned to a familiar rhythm for the children. They missed their tree deeply, often finding themselves thinking about the times they had shared beneath its branches and the memories they had made together. Each of them held onto their piece of the garden as a reminder, and whenever they looked at the flowers, soil, or mementos they had taken, they felt a mixture of warmth and sadness. They knew that while the Friendship Tree was gone, its presence lingered in their hearts and in the bond they shared.

One sunny afternoon, the children met at Samira's house, enjoying the warm weather as they sat together in her backyard. They talked about school, about their summer plans, and about the new projects they were each working on. But as the conversation grew quiet, they found themselves once again reflecting on the Friendship Tree, its absence casting a subtle shadow over their gathering. It was clear that each of them felt the gap left by the tree, a reminder of the special place it had held in their friendship.

Leo, who always had a knack for breaking silences, cleared his throat and spoke up. "I've been thinking," he said, his eyes thoughtful. "Maybe it's time for us to plant something new. Not to replace the Friendship Tree, because nothing ever could. But maybe we could plant something as a way to keep moving forward."

The others looked at him, intrigued by the idea. They realized that while they had each kept something from the garden, they hadn't considered creating something new together. The thought of planting another tree or starting a new garden didn't feel like replacing the Friendship Tree—it felt like a way to honor it, to let its memory grow into something new. They agreed that planting something together would be a beautiful way to channel their love for the tree and continue the legacy it had left behind.

Elara suggested that they plant the new tree in a different location, somewhere that felt special but was less likely to be affected by future park changes. They discussed a few options, considering places they all enjoyed and that would be meaningful for them. After some debate, they decided on a small patch of land near the edge of the park, close to a quiet, grassy area that had a clear view of the nearby hills. The spot felt peaceful and safe, and they imagined that a new tree planted there could grow without interference, its roots digging deep and strong.

With their plan in place, they spent the next few days gathering everything they needed for the planting. Samira brought some of the soil she had kept from the original garden, thinking it would be a meaningful way to connect the new tree to the old one. Leo found a small tree sapling at a local nursery, a young maple tree with delicate leaves that reminded them of the early days of the Friendship Tree. Elara researched the best way to plant and care for the sapling, making sure they knew how to give it the best chance to grow. And Liam brought small stones from his backyard, which they planned to place around the base of the tree, just as they had done with the Friendship Tree, marking it as their own.

The day of the planting arrived, and the children felt a mix of excitement and nostalgia as they walked to the chosen spot in the park. They had told their families about their plan, and a few parents and siblings had come to watch, offering words of encouragement and support. As they approached the spot where they would plant the new tree, they felt a sense of calm and purpose, as though they were continuing a journey that had begun long ago.

They dug a hole in the ground, working together to make it just the right size for the young tree. When they were ready, Leo carefully placed the sapling in the hole, positioning it so that it stood tall and straight. Samira sprinkled a bit of the soil from the old garden around the base, her movements slow and deliberate. The others followed suit, each of them adding a handful of soil, feeling a quiet connection to the past as they brought a part of the old garden into the new one. As they worked, they shared memories of the Friendship Tree, each story adding to the atmosphere of love and unity that surrounded them.

Once the tree was firmly planted, they arranged the stones Liam had brought in a circle around the base, creating a small barrier that marked it as theirs. They stepped back, admiring their work, feeling a sense of accomplishment and joy. The young tree looked fragile, its branches thin and delicate, but they knew that with time, it would grow strong and tall, just as the Friendship Tree had. They hoped that this tree would become a symbol of new beginnings, a reminder that even after loss, there was always room for growth.

As they stood around the tree, Samira suggested that they each make a wish for its future. She explained that by putting their hopes and dreams into the tree, they would be giving it the strength to grow, just as they had with the Friendship Tree. They all agreed, touched by the idea, and took turns sharing their wishes aloud.

Leo went first, his voice filled with determination. "I wish that this tree will grow big and strong, so that it can be a place where others can come to feel safe and happy, just like we did with the Friendship Tree." The others nodded, touched by his words, feeling a renewed sense of purpose in their new tree.

Samira spoke next, her voice soft and full of warmth. "I wish that this tree will remind people of friendship and love, that it will be a place where people can come together, even if they're different. I hope it brings joy to everyone who visits it."

Elara took her turn, her gaze steady as she looked at the tree. "I wish that this tree will teach others the lessons we learned from the Friendship Tree—about patience, kindness, and growth. I hope it becomes a symbol of strength and resilience."

Finally, Liam, who had been quiet but thoughtful, placed his hand on the young tree. "I wish that this tree will remind us to keep growing, even when things get hard. I hope it stands tall and proud, no matter what challenges it faces."

After sharing their wishes, they each placed a hand on the tree, feeling a sense of unity and hope as they stood together. They knew that this new tree was a continuation of their journey, a way to carry forward the love and memories they had created around the Friendship Tree. The sapling might not be the same as the old tree, but it was a part of them now, a symbol of their friendship, resilience, and commitment to one another.

As they sat down together around the tree, enjoying the quiet beauty of the park, they talked about the future, imagining all the ways the tree might grow and change. They spoke about coming back each year to check on its progress, about adding to the garden around it, and about sharing its story with others who might find inspiration in its journey. They knew that this tree, like their friendship, would grow slowly, changing with each season, but they were ready for the journey, excited to see where it would take them.

In the days that followed, they returned often to check on the young tree, watering it and tending to it with the same care they had shown the Friendship Tree. They noticed each new leaf, each small sign of growth, and celebrated every milestone. They found joy in the process, feeling a sense of fulfillment as they watched the tree slowly take root and grow stronger.

Over time, they began to think of the new tree not as a replacement, but as a continuation of the Friendship Tree's legacy. It was a reminder that life moved forward, that even after loss, there was always room for new beginnings. They felt a deep sense of peace, knowing that the spirit of the Friendship Tree lived on, not only in their memories but in the roots of the new tree they had planted together.

And as they gathered around the young tree, laughing and sharing stories, they realized that their friendship, like the tree, would continue to grow, grounded in love, resilience, and the lessons they had learned together. They had planted new seeds, not only in the earth but in their hearts, seeds that would grow and flourish, shaping their lives and their friendship in ways they could only begin to imagine.

Chapter 17: The Gift of Passing It On

Summer had settled fully over the town, bringing long days filled with warmth and the sounds of laughter in the park. The children visited their newly planted tree often, watching as it slowly grew stronger, its leaves greener and fuller with each passing week. Their visits to the tree became a ritual, a chance for them to sit together and talk about their lives, their dreams, and the memories they had shared under the Friendship Tree. While the new tree was still young and fragile, it had become a source of joy for them, a symbol of their friendship and their journey together.

One sunny afternoon, as they gathered under its branches, they noticed a group of younger children playing nearby. The younger kids were laughing and running, weaving in and out between trees, chasing each other in a game of tag. As the children watched, they felt a wave of nostalgia wash over them, remembering their own early days in the park, the games they had played together, and the way they had first come together around the Friendship Tree.

Elara, who was watching the younger kids with a thoughtful expression, turned to her friends and said, "Do you remember when we used to play like that? Back when we didn't know this tree or the Friendship Tree would mean so much to us?" Her words made them all smile, each of them recalling those carefree early days. They had come so far since then, and the tree had been with them through it all, growing alongside their friendship.

Leo, always eager for a new idea, perked up. "What if we invited the younger kids over and shared the story of the Friendship Tree with them?" he suggested. "Maybe it could become something special for them too, like it is for us." The others looked at him with excitement, loving the idea of passing on the story and sharing the legacy of the Friendship Tree with a new generation. They knew that the tree had brought so much joy, wisdom, and growth into their lives, and the thought of sharing that with others filled them with a sense of purpose and pride.

They waited until the younger children had finished their game before approaching them. Smiling warmly, Elara introduced their group, and the younger kids, who had seen them around the park before, looked at them with curiosity and admiration. "We wanted to share a story with you," Elara began, her voice gentle but filled with excitement. "It's about a tree that meant a lot to us, a tree that brought us together and taught us so much. We call it the Friendship Tree."

The younger children gathered around, their faces filled with wonder as they listened. Samira, always expressive, added details about how the Friendship Tree had started as a small sapling, how they had brought soil from their homes to plant it together, and how they had created a garden around it filled with items that represented each of them. She shared stories of their adventures, the festivals they had held, and the quiet moments spent together under its branches. The younger kids listened with wide eyes, captivated by the magic of the story.

As they continued sharing, Leo explained how the Friendship Tree had been a place where they learned important lessons about patience, kindness, and resilience. He told them about the time they had worked to protect it from storms and about how it had been a place of comfort and strength for them during difficult times. Liam, usually quiet, spoke up as well, sharing how the tree had taught him the value of listening, of being present, and of appreciating the beauty in small things.

The younger children were clearly enchanted by the story, their eyes shining with excitement and curiosity. One of them, a girl with curly hair and a bright smile, asked, "Can we help take care of this tree too? Can we make it our Friendship Tree?" Her question brought smiles to the older children's faces. They had hoped that the story would inspire the younger kids, and now, seeing the eagerness in their faces, they felt a sense of fulfillment and joy. The tree they had planted together was not only a symbol of their own friendship but could now become a source of connection and meaning for others as well.

The older children welcomed the younger kids to join them in caring for the tree. They taught them how to water it properly, how to check for any signs of damage, and even shared stories of the little traditions they had created around the Friendship Tree. They encouraged the younger children to add their own items to the garden if they wished—small things that represented their personalities, dreams, or even just simple tokens of love for the tree.

Over the following weeks, the younger children returned regularly to visit the tree, often bringing small gifts for the garden. Some brought painted rocks, others brought flowers, and one even brought a tiny carved heart made of wood, which she placed carefully at the base of the tree. The garden around the new tree began to grow richer and more colorful, each item a reminder of the friendships forming around it, a continuation of the legacy started by the original Friendship Tree.

The older children watched with pride and joy as the younger kids formed their own connection with the tree. They could see the same excitement and curiosity in the younger children's eyes that they had once felt themselves, and it filled them with a sense of peace and fulfillment. They realized that by passing on the story of the Friendship Tree, they were creating a ripple effect, a legacy of kindness, unity, and love that would continue to grow and spread through the park.

One day, as they were all gathered around the tree, one of the younger children asked them what they had learned from the Friendship Tree. The older children exchanged glances, realizing that they each had so much to share. Taking turns, they explained how the tree had taught them patience, how it had shown them that growth took time and that beautiful things couldn't be rushed. They talked about resilience, about how the tree had stood strong through storms and how they had learned to face challenges together, supporting one another through difficult times.

They also shared lessons about kindness and empathy, explaining how the tree had become a place of comfort for them, a reminder to treat each other with understanding and compassion. They spoke about the importance of unity, of how each of their differences had made their friendship stronger, just as each branch of the tree added to its beauty and strength. The younger children listened intently, absorbing the wisdom and lessons with open hearts, their admiration for the older children growing with each story.

The younger children began to come to the tree on their own, bringing their friends and even family members to show them the garden and share the story of the Friendship Tree. The tree became a gathering place for the whole community, a place where people could come together, share their stories, and find comfort and inspiration. It was no longer just the Friendship Tree of the original group; it had become a symbol of connection and unity for everyone who visited it.

Chapter 18: A Lesson in Letting Go

As the seasons changed, the children's lives grew busier, filled with new responsibilities, challenges, and exciting opportunities. They were growing up, and with that came changes that none of them could have predicted. Schoolwork became more demanding, and each of them had different commitments and hobbies that took up much of their time. Their schedules no longer aligned as perfectly as they once had, and gradually, their visits to the park and the Friendship Tree became less frequent.

One crisp autumn afternoon, Elara found herself walking through the park alone, something she hadn't done in a long time. She hadn't planned to visit the Friendship Tree that day, but as she strolled along the familiar path, memories of the times she'd spent there with her friends washed over her. She stopped by the tree, noticing how much it had grown since they first planted it. Its branches were fuller, stretching out as if embracing the sky, and the leaves were a vibrant mix of orange and red, a sign of the changing season. She ran her hand along the bark, feeling the rough texture beneath her fingers, and a bittersweet feeling settled in her heart.

It wasn't long before she was joined by Samira, who had come to the park for some inspiration for her latest art project. Samira's face lit up when she saw Elara by the tree, and they embraced, laughing at the coincidence of meeting there. They sat down together, talking about school, family, and all the little things that had been keeping them busy. They hadn't realized just how much they had missed spending time at the tree, and being there brought a sense of peace and comfort that was both familiar and precious.

As they talked, Leo and Liam arrived, each of them surprised to see the others there. They exchanged stories of their busy lives, their new interests, and the challenges they were facing, grateful for the chance to reconnect. Sitting together under the tree felt like a return to something deeply important, and they found themselves reminiscing about the memories they had made there, each story bringing laughter and a touch of nostalgia.

But as they shared stories, a quiet realization settled over them—they were no longer the same kids who had planted the Friendship Tree. They had grown and changed in ways they hadn't anticipated, and though their bond was still strong, they could feel the subtle shifts in their friendship. They weren't drifting apart, but their lives were pulling them in different directions, and they each felt the weight of that reality.

Elara, who was usually calm and thoughtful, spoke up, her voice gentle but steady. "I think it's okay if things change," she said, looking around at her friends. "We'll always have the Friendship Tree, and we'll always have the memories we made here. But maybe it's time to let go a little, to accept that we're all growing in different ways."

Her words struck a chord with the others. They knew that change was natural, that growing up meant embracing new paths and discovering new parts of themselves. But hearing it aloud made it feel real in a way they hadn't acknowledged before. It was a difficult realization, but they understood that letting go didn't mean losing what they had—it meant allowing it to evolve, to become something new.

They spent a long time sitting in silence, each of them reflecting on what the Friendship Tree had meant to them and the lessons it had taught them. They remembered the festivals, the games, the challenges they had faced together, and the laughter they had shared. They realized that every moment spent at the Friendship Tree had shaped them, helping them grow into the people they were becoming. And though they felt a pang of sadness at the thought of moving forward, they also felt a sense of gratitude for everything the tree and their friendship had given them.

To mark this moment of transition, they decided to leave something behind, a small token of their love and appreciation for the tree. They each took out a small object—a drawing, a rock, a pressed flower, a handwritten note—and placed it at the base of the tree, creating a circle of memories that would stay there, even as they moved on. It was their way of saying thank you, of honoring the tree and the friendship it had helped nurture.

As they stood back and looked at the circle of mementos, they felt a sense of closure. They knew that life would continue to pull them in different directions, but they also knew that the Friendship Tree would always be there, a reminder of the journey they had shared. They promised each other to visit when they could, to come back and check on the tree, to let it be a symbol of their enduring connection, even if they couldn't be together as often as they once had.

In the days that followed, they each returned to their lives, carrying the lessons of the Friendship Tree in their hearts. They learned to let go with grace, to appreciate the beauty of change, and to embrace the new paths opening up before them. And though they missed the simplicity of their days at the tree, they found comfort in knowing that their friendship had been built on a foundation of love, respect, and shared memories that would last a lifetime.

Each of them grew in their own way. Elara found herself drawn to environmental activism, inspired by the care she had shown for the Friendship Tree and her desire to protect the natural world. Samira pursued her passion for art with a new sense of purpose, incorporating elements of nature and friendship into her work, sharing the beauty of her memories with the world. Leo embraced his adventurous spirit, exploring new hobbies and pushing his limits, carrying with him the lessons of resilience and strength he had learned from the tree. And Liam, ever calm and steady, found comfort in nature, often visiting the park alone, where he would sit quietly under the branches, finding peace in the presence of the tree that had taught him so much.

They each visited the Friendship Tree from time to time, though rarely together. On those visits, they would sit beneath its branches, reflecting on the memories they had made and the lessons they had learned. They would see the circle of mementos at its base, a reminder of the bond they had shared, and feel a quiet joy knowing that, no matter where life took them, the tree would always hold a piece of their friendship.

As the years passed, the Friendship Tree grew taller and stronger, its branches spreading wide, casting shade over the park as it had always done. It became a landmark, a beloved part of the community, where new generations came to play, laugh, and find comfort. And though the original group of friends was no longer there every day, their presence remained in the roots of the tree, in the memories woven into its branches, and in the love that had helped it grow.

Chapter 19: The Circle Reunited

Years had passed since the children had first planted the Friendship Tree. Their lives had grown in ways they could never have imagined back then, filled with new adventures, challenges, and dreams. They had each found their own path, moving to different towns and pursuing their passions, but the memories of the Friendship Tree and the times they had spent together remained a constant in their hearts. They still thought of each other often, wondering how their friends were doing and occasionally sending letters or messages to stay in touch. Though they were separated by distance, their bond had never truly faded.

One summer, a letter arrived in each of their mailboxes, inviting them to return to their hometown for a special gathering. The letter was handwritten, with the familiar looping handwriting of Elara. She had written to tell them about a community event that was being held in honor of the park where they had once spent so much time. The town had decided to create a new garden area near the Friendship Tree, and Elara thought it would be the perfect opportunity for them to reunite. She mentioned that the Friendship Tree had grown taller and stronger over the years, a beloved symbol in the park that now held countless memories for people of all ages. Elara suggested that they gather by the tree to reconnect, to see how much it had grown, and to celebrate the memories they had created.

Each of them felt a wave of excitement and nostalgia as they read the letter. It had been years since they had all been together, and the thought of returning to the tree filled them with anticipation. They remembered their last gathering under the tree, the promises they had made, and the circle of mementos they had left as a tribute to their friendship. They knew this reunion would be different; they were no longer children, but young adults with lives of their own. Yet, deep down, they knew that the Friendship Tree would always be a part of them, connecting them across time and distance.

When the day of the gathering arrived, the park was bustling with people, each enjoying the warm, sunny afternoon. Families picnicked on the grass, children laughed as they played on the swings, and friends gathered under shady trees. The air was filled with the scent of flowers, and the sounds of cheerful voices echoed through the park. The atmosphere was lively and vibrant, a reflection of the community that had grown around the Friendship Tree.

Elara was the first to arrive, standing by the tree with a mixture of excitement and nervousness. She hadn't seen her friends in years, and though they had kept in touch, she wondered if time and distance had changed them. She gazed up at the tree, marveling at how tall and strong it had become, its branches stretching wide as if welcoming her back. The circle of mementos they had left years before was still there, a little weathered by time but unmistakable—a testament to their friendship that had endured even as they had grown.

Soon, she saw a familiar figure approaching. Samira walked towards her, a broad smile lighting up her face as she waved. The two friends embraced, laughing with joy as they marveled at how much each of them had changed and yet remained the same. Samira pointed out a small paintbrush she had placed by the tree years ago, a symbol of her love for art that had now blossomed into a career. She told Elara about her work as an artist, how she used the memories of the Friendship Tree and their time together as inspiration in her paintings. Elara listened with pride, feeling as though a piece of their childhood had come to life through Samira's passion.

Moments later, Leo arrived, his familiar grin and boundless energy still intact, though he had grown taller and more confident. He embraced his friends, sharing stories of his travels and the adventures he had taken on, each one more daring than the last. He laughed as he recalled their old days of climbing trees and exploring the park, admitting that those simple childhood adventures had sparked his love for exploration. He showed them a small compass he had left in the circle, now weathered and worn, a reminder of the adventurous spirit he had carried with him all these years.

Finally, Liam arrived, quieter than the others but with a warm smile that conveyed his happiness to be reunited with his friends. He walked over to the tree, touching the bark and closing his eyes for a moment, as if reconnecting with an old friend. Liam shared how he had found peace and fulfillment in nature, working in environmental conservation to protect the forests and green spaces that had always brought him a sense of calm. He pointed to a small wooden carving of a leaf that he had left by the tree, a symbol of his quiet strength and love for the natural world.

As they stood together under the Friendship Tree, they felt a wave of nostalgia wash over them, each memory vivid and alive. They laughed as they recounted their adventures, from the festivals and games to the challenges they had overcome. They shared stories of the lessons they had learned from the tree, the moments of growth, and the wisdom that had shaped who they were. Each of them had been influenced by their time at the Friendship Tree in different ways, but the lessons they had learned together had become a part of who they were.

After sharing their stories, they sat down in a circle under the tree, each of them feeling a profound sense of connection to their friends and to the place that had been the foundation of their friendship. They noticed that some of the younger children in the park had gathered nearby, watching them with curious eyes, much like they had once done with older kids who had shared stories with them. Elara invited them over, and the children eagerly joined, sitting around the group as they listened to the story of the Friendship Tree.

As they shared the tale, they realized that their story had become more than just a memory—it had become a legacy, something they could pass down to a new generation. They told the younger children about the importance of friendship, of caring for one another and for the places that held special meaning. They shared the lessons they had learned about patience, resilience, kindness, and the value of coming together despite their differences. The children listened, wide-eyed and captivated, each of them feeling the magic of the story and the sense of wonder that surrounded the Friendship Tree.

When the story was finished, one of the younger children asked if they could add something to the circle of mementos. The friends exchanged a glance, smiling as they realized that the tree's legacy was continuing, growing through the lives of new people who would come to love and care for it just as they had. They watched as the children carefully placed small items in the circle—a toy, a drawing, a flower, each one representing their hopes and dreams, their own unique contribution to the tree's story.

As the day drew to a close, the friends stood together one last time, feeling a deep sense of peace and fulfillment. They knew that they would always carry the memories of the Friendship Tree with them, but they also understood that they were part of something larger. Their friendship, their shared memories, and the lessons they had learned had woven themselves into the fabric of the community, becoming a lasting presence that would inspire others for generations to come.

Chapter 20: Seasons of Friendship

As years continued to pass, the Friendship Tree grew taller and sturdier, becoming a cherished part of the park. Generations came and went, each adding to the legacy of the tree. It stood as a symbol of endurance and friendship, its branches spreading wide, casting shade over those who gathered beneath it. For those who visited the park, the Friendship Tree became a place to pause, to reflect, and to connect. People would sit under its canopy on sunny days, leaning against its thick trunk, reading, drawing, or just watching the world around them. For the town, it became a place where memories were made, secrets were shared, and lives intertwined.

The original group of friends, who had once been inseparable, found themselves scattered across different cities and countries. Each of them had pursued their dreams, built careers, and, in some cases, started families. They still stayed in touch, exchanging messages and calls when they could, sharing updates on their lives and reminiscing about the past. The Friendship Tree remained a central topic of their conversations, and they often wondered how much it had changed and grown. It held a timeless place in their hearts, a part of their shared history that nothing could replace.

One summer, Elara decided to visit her hometown with her family. She hadn't been back in years, and she felt a mix of excitement and nostalgia as she walked through the familiar streets. Her children, who had heard countless stories about the Friendship Tree, were eager to see it in person. Elara was filled with a sense of joy as she led them to the park, pointing out landmarks from her childhood, sharing memories of the games she'd played and the adventures she'd had with her friends.

When they reached the Friendship Tree, Elara felt a rush of emotions. The tree was even taller and more majestic than she remembered, its branches reaching out as if welcoming her back. She could see the familiar circle of mementos at its base, though now it was surrounded by new items left by people who had come to love the tree over the years. There were colorful rocks, small toys, and even a few handwritten notes tucked into the crevices of the bark. It was clear that the tree had become more than just a landmark—it was a living testament to the connections it had inspired.

Elara's children ran to the tree, touching its trunk with wonder, their eyes wide with excitement. She smiled as she watched them, feeling a sense of pride that her stories had sparked their curiosity and love for the tree. As they explored, she sat down beneath the branches, leaning back against the trunk and letting the memories of her own childhood wash over her. It felt like coming home, a return to a place that had been a constant source of strength and comfort throughout her life.

Later that day, she sent a message to her old friends, telling them about her visit to the Friendship Tree and sharing photos of her children playing around it. Her message brought a wave of responses, each friend expressing their own nostalgia and longing to visit the tree again. They talked about how the tree had grown, how it had changed, and how it still held a special place in their hearts. The conversation rekindled memories, and soon they were reminiscing about their days spent at the park, laughing about the adventures they'd had and the lessons they'd learned together.

Inspired by their conversation, Elara suggested that they plan a reunion, inviting their families to join them so they could share the legacy of the Friendship Tree with a new generation. The idea excited them, and over the next few months, they coordinated their schedules, making arrangements to return to their hometown for a long-awaited gathering.

When the day of the reunion arrived, the park was filled with laughter and chatter as the friends and their families gathered under the Friendship Tree. For many of them, it was the first time their children had met, and the sight of the next generation playing together around the tree brought a sense of joy and fulfillment. The children listened intently as their parents told stories about their childhood, sharing memories of the tree, the games they'd played, and the lessons they'd learned. For the younger ones, it was like a fairy tale come to life—a tree that had watched over their parents and had now become a part of their own lives.

As the friends caught up, they marveled at how much had changed and yet how familiar everything felt. They talked about their lives, their dreams, and the paths they had taken. Each of them had been shaped by their time at the Friendship Tree, and though they had grown in different ways, the values and lessons they had learned remained with them. They felt a deep sense of gratitude for the friendship they had shared, for the experiences that had brought them together, and for the tree that had been a witness to it all.

Chapter 21: A New Seed

As time went on, the original friends' lives continued to evolve, each of them finding new challenges and joys in the paths they'd chosen. Though their individual journeys had led them in different directions, their connection to the Friendship Tree remained a powerful thread that wove through the fabric of their lives. The tree had become more than a memory; it was a symbol of strength and unity, a reminder of the bond they had formed through shared moments and lessons learned together.

One spring, Samira returned to her hometown with a specific purpose in mind. She had been thinking about the Friendship Tree and how it had influenced her life in countless ways, from the friendships she had cherished to the creativity it had sparked in her art. She wanted to give something back, something that would continue the tree's legacy in a way that reached beyond her circle of friends and the town. As she walked through the park one sunny afternoon, memories washed over her—the games they'd played, the conversations they'd shared, and the dreams they'd nurtured under the tree's branches. She felt a renewed appreciation for the impact the Friendship Tree had had on her life and on her friends.

With the idea of giving back to her community, Samira approached the town council with a proposal. She wanted to create an art project centered around the Friendship Tree, something that would celebrate the values of unity, growth, and kindness. Her vision was to paint a mural on one of the park's walls, a vibrant representation of the tree, its branches stretching across the wall with leaves of every color imaginable. She hoped that the mural would inspire others to find joy and strength in friendship, and perhaps even encourage new friendships to blossom within the park.

The town council was enthusiastic about her idea, and after some planning, they agreed to provide the support and resources needed to bring her vision to life. Samira spent weeks designing the mural, each brushstroke and color carefully chosen to reflect the spirit of the Friendship Tree. She included symbols of her friends, incorporating small details that represented each of them, their unique qualities woven into the branches and leaves of the tree. She added elements of nature, such as birds and butterflies, to signify freedom and growth, and she left space for future generations to add their own marks, allowing the mural to grow along with the community.

On the day Samira began painting, families and friends gathered in the park, curious to see the mural take shape. The atmosphere was filled with excitement and anticipation, and as Samira started painting, she felt a sense of purpose and joy. People stopped by to watch, to ask questions, and to share their own memories of the Friendship Tree. Some told stories of meeting friends or loved ones by the tree, others shared memories of childhood days spent playing in the park, and a few even spoke of the inspiration they'd found under its branches. Samira listened to each story with gratitude, feeling as though the tree's legacy had extended far beyond her group of friends.

As she painted, she felt connected not only to the tree and her friends, but also to everyone who had ever visited the park, everyone who had been touched by the tree's presence. The mural became a tapestry of stories, a living piece of art that celebrated the connections people had made and the lessons they had learned from the Friendship Tree. As she painted, she thought of her friends, of the memories they had shared, and of the way each of them had carried the tree's lessons into their lives. She knew they would be proud of the mural, proud that the tree's legacy would continue to inspire others.

Word of the mural spread quickly, and soon, people from all over the town, and even nearby communities, came to see it. They marveled at the vibrant colors and intricate details, each leaf and branch telling a story of friendship and unity. Children, in particular, were drawn to the mural, running their hands over the painted leaves and pointing out the animals hidden in its branches. Samira encouraged them to add their own touches, handing out brushes and inviting them to paint their own symbols and shapes, making the mural a collaborative creation.

One day, as she was working on the final details of the mural, Elara and Leo surprised her with a visit. They had heard about her project and wanted to see it for themselves. They were in awe as they took in the mural, each detail bringing back memories of their time together, of the lessons they had learned, and the love they had shared under the Friendship Tree. They hugged Samira, thanking her for creating something so beautiful, something that would inspire others to cherish friendship and community.

As they stood together, gazing at the mural, a group of children approached, watching them with curiosity. Elara knelt down and began telling them the story of the Friendship Tree, explaining how it had brought her and her friends together, how it had taught them about kindness, patience, and resilience. The children listened with wide eyes, clearly captivated by the story, and when Elara finished, they asked if they could add something to the mural. Samira handed them brushes, smiling as they carefully painted small symbols and patterns, adding their own contributions to the tree's legacy.

The mural quickly became a beloved part of the park, a place where people gathered to admire its beauty, to reflect on their own friendships, and to share stories with each other. It became a symbol of the community's unity, a reminder that the bonds they formed would carry them through life's challenges, just as the Friendship Tree had done for Samira and her friends. Over time, the mural grew, with new additions from people who visited the park, each brushstroke a mark of love and connection.

Through her work on the mural, Samira felt a deep sense of fulfillment, knowing that she had given something meaningful to her community, something that would carry on the values of the Friendship Tree for generations to come. The mural became her way of honoring her friends, of expressing her gratitude for the memories they had made, and of sharing the tree's legacy with others.

One afternoon, as Samira was adding a final layer to the mural, she saw Liam standing nearby, watching her with a quiet smile. He walked over, admiring her work, and they spent a long time talking about the tree, about the lessons it had taught them, and about the ways it had shaped their lives. Liam shared how the tree's lessons on resilience and patience had guided him in his work, reminding him of the importance of caring for the environment and for the people around him. They both felt a deep sense of gratitude for the tree, for the lessons it had taught them, and for the bond it had created.

As they finished talking, Liam took out a small sapling he had brought with him. It was a young tree, delicate and green, with tiny leaves that swayed in the gentle breeze. He explained that he wanted to plant it near the mural, as a way of continuing the Friendship Tree's legacy, of creating a new place where people could gather, connect, and learn from each other. Samira loved the idea, and together, they planted the sapling, feeling a renewed sense of hope and purpose as they placed it in the earth.

The new tree quickly became a gathering place, much like the Friendship Tree had once been. People came to sit under its shade, to share stories, and to add their own marks to the mural. The park became a place of connection, a place where people from all walks of life came together to celebrate friendship and community. The mural and the new tree stood side by side, symbols of growth, unity, and love, reminders of the enduring power of connection.

Over time, the mural became known as the "Friendship Wall," a beloved part of the community that drew people from near and far. Each person who visited left a piece of themselves behind, adding to the tapestry of stories, symbols, and colors. The wall and the tree grew together, becoming a living legacy that carried forward the values of the

Friendship Tree, inspiring others to find joy, strength, and connection in the world around them.

For Samira, Elara, Leo, and Liam, the mural and the new tree became a reminder of their own journey, of the friendships that had shaped them, and of the memories they held dear. They knew that the tree's legacy would continue to inspire others, that its lessons would be carried forward by everyone who visited the park, everyone who sat under its branches or added to the wall. They felt a sense of peace, knowing that the spirit of the Friendship Tree would live on, a testament to the power of friendship, unity, and love.

Chapter 22: The Tree of Many Stories

The Friendship Tree, now a towering presence in the park, had become an irreplaceable part of the town's landscape. Its branches stretched wide, casting shade and offering shelter to everyone who came near. The community mural, affectionately called the "Friendship Wall," stood nearby, alive with colors and symbols that had been added over the years. Together, the tree and the wall represented the spirit of the town—a place where people from all walks of life came to connect, reflect, and share a part of themselves.

For Samira, Elara, Leo, and Liam, the tree and wall had become symbols of a shared journey that had shaped them and enriched their lives. They visited whenever they could, each time finding something new, a new story added to the wall, a new symbol painted with care, or an unexpected note of gratitude left at the tree's base. These additions created a vibrant tapestry that spoke of countless friendships, hopes, dreams, and lessons learned. The tree had grown to symbolize not just their own memories but the collective memories of the entire community.

One warm summer evening, the friends decided to meet at the park for a gathering, bringing their families and friends to share in the beauty of the tree and the wall. It had become a beloved tradition, something they looked forward to each year. As they approached the tree, they were greeted by familiar faces and new ones alike, each person drawn by the legacy that the Friendship Tree represented. The air was filled with laughter, voices mingling as people shared stories and memories of their own connections to the tree.

That evening, Elara suggested that everyone present share a story or memory related to the tree. It was a spontaneous idea, inspired by the thought that the Friendship Tree was a gathering place, a living symbol of unity, where stories could be shared and preserved. She felt that by sharing these memories aloud, they could each contribute a piece of their own journey to the collective legacy that the tree had become.

One by one, people began sharing their stories. Some spoke of friendships that had started under the tree, moments when a simple greeting turned into a lifelong connection. Others talked about difficult times they had faced, describing how the quiet shade of the tree had offered them a place of solace, a reminder that they were never truly alone. Parents shared memories of bringing their children to the park, of watching them play and explore, and how the tree had been a constant presence through each stage of their lives.

A young woman stepped forward, her eyes bright with emotion as she held a small notebook in her hands. She explained that she had come to the park every week for the past year, using the shade of the tree as a place to write down her dreams, her fears, and her hopes for the future. She shared how the act of writing at the base of the tree had helped her find clarity, how the tree had become a place where she could be honest with herself, away from the demands of daily life. Her story resonated with the group, and they thanked her for sharing something so personal, recognizing the importance of having a place to reflect and grow.

As more stories were shared, the friends noticed that the tree had touched people in ways they hadn't expected. For some, it had been a place of quiet reflection; for others, it had been a source of inspiration. A group of children shared their story about creating a "secret club" under the tree, complete with a set of rules they had written and hidden in a small tin box at its base. They laughed as they recounted their adventures, their faces lighting up with excitement. The adults chuckled, reminded of their own childhood days and the sense of wonder that the tree had sparked in them.

As the night went on, Leo shared a story from his own past, recalling a time when he had been uncertain about the path he wanted to take in life. He spoke about how he had come to the tree alone one evening, feeling lost and unsure, and how sitting under its branches had given him a sense of calm, a feeling that everything would be okay. He described how the tree had reminded him of his friends, of the lessons they had shared, and how it had given him the courage to pursue his dreams. His story touched everyone, reminding them of the power of friendship and the importance of having a place to find peace and clarity.

Liam spoke next, sharing how the tree had influenced his decision to work in environmental conservation. He explained that the tree had taught him the value of protecting natural spaces, of ensuring that future generations could experience the same sense of wonder and connection he had felt as a child. He spoke passionately about the importance of preserving green spaces and about the joy he felt in knowing that the tree had inspired him to pursue a life dedicated to nature. His story sparked a sense of appreciation for the tree's role as a teacher, a silent guide that had shaped the lives of those who had come to love it.

One of the last people to share was an elderly man who had been watching quietly from the edge of the gathering. He stepped forward slowly, his voice gentle but filled with warmth. He shared that he had lived in the town for most of his life and that he had watched the tree grow from a small sapling to the magnificent presence it was now. He explained how the tree had been a part of his life through many stages—when he was a young man, newly married, when he had become a father, and now, as a grandfather. He spoke about how he brought his grandchildren to the park, showing them the tree and sharing stories of his own. His words reminded everyone that the tree was not just a symbol of friendship, but a testament to the passage of time, to the resilience and beauty of nature that could endure across generations.

As the evening drew to a close, the group gathered in a circle around the tree, each person feeling a renewed sense of connection to one another and to the tree itself. They had come together to share stories, to laugh, to remember, and to celebrate the tree that had become an anchor in their lives. They realized that the tree was not just a part of their past, but a living symbol of their present, a reminder of the friendships they had formed, the lessons they had learned, and the love they had shared.

Before they left, each person took a moment to add a new memento to the base of the tree. Some placed stones they had collected, others left handwritten notes or small trinkets, each item a tribute to the impact the tree had had on their lives. The circle of mementos grew that night, expanding with symbols of love, friendship, and gratitude. It was a reminder that the tree's legacy would continue, that it would grow with each new story, each new person who came to share in its shade.

Chapter 23: A Legacy Renewed

As the years continued to pass, the Friendship Tree had become an icon, not just for the town but for neighboring communities as well. The town's park, once a quiet place with only a few visitors, had blossomed into a cherished gathering ground, largely due to the presence of the tree and the mural nearby. People came from all around to see the mural and to sit beneath the Friendship Tree's expansive branches, adding their own memories, hopes, and tokens to the circle that surrounded its base. The tree had become more than just a symbol; it was a living monument to kindness, connection, and unity.

One spring, an unexpected announcement was made by the town council: the park was going to undergo renovations. The goal was to enhance the park with more amenities, to make it accessible for everyone, and to protect the areas that had become sacred to the community. The Friendship Tree was a central part of these plans, and the town council wanted to ensure that it was preserved, even as they made the park more accommodating. The council, recognizing the importance of the Friendship Tree to the town, decided to gather input from the community to find ways to protect it and enhance its legacy for future generations.

The council invited townspeople to a meeting to discuss the upcoming changes, and the turnout was unprecedented. People of all ages, from young children to elderly residents, filled the town hall, each of them eager to voice their thoughts on the Friendship Tree and how they could help protect it. There was an undeniable energy in the room, a shared determination to preserve the tree and the mural that had become the heart of the park. Elara, Leo, Samira, and Liam, who had all returned to town for the meeting, were overwhelmed by the community's devotion to the tree and to the legacy they had unknowingly set in motion so many years before.

One by one, people stood up to share their stories and ideas. Some spoke of the tree's role as a place of solace, where they had come during difficult times to find comfort and peace. Others talked about the friendships they had formed there, the moments of joy they had experienced, and the ways in which the tree had become part of their own family traditions. Each story added depth to the tree's legacy, and the council listened intently, moved by the passion and love expressed by every speaker.

Elara, who had been deeply moved by the stories, suggested creating a series of plaques to commemorate the different experiences people had shared with the tree. Each plaque could contain a short story, a memory, or a quote from someone whose life had been touched by the tree. The plaques could be placed in a circle around the tree, creating a walkway that celebrated the tree's impact on the community. The idea was met with enthusiasm, and the council agreed to include it in their plans.

Samira, inspired by Elara's suggestion, proposed adding a small pavilion near the tree. It could serve as a gathering space for events, story-telling, and seasonal celebrations, ensuring that the tree continued to be a place of unity and joy. Leo suggested that they add a small garden around the pavilion, planting flowers from various regions to symbolize the diversity of people who came to the park. He envisioned a mix of colors and fragrances that would make the tree and mural a focal point of beauty and serenity in the park. His idea added a new dimension to the project, and the council readily agreed to incorporate the garden into their plans.

Liam, who had spent years working in environmental conservation, reminded the group that the tree's health needed to be prioritized, especially as the park underwent renovations. He proposed that a dedicated team of local botanists and arborists be assigned to monitor the tree, to ensure that it remained healthy and strong through the construction and beyond. His suggestion was warmly received, and the council promised to consult with specialists to create a preservation plan that would safeguard the tree's well-being.

With these ideas in mind, the community set to work on bringing the plans to life. A team of volunteers, including Elara, Leo, Samira, and Liam, worked tirelessly alongside local artisans, gardeners, and town officials. Over the next few months, the area around the Friendship Tree transformed, evolving into a beautiful space that honored the tree's history while making room for new stories to be created. The pavilion was built, a graceful wooden structure with open sides that allowed the natural beauty of the park to be seen from every angle. The circle of plaques was installed, each one a tribute to a person or family whose lives had been touched by the Friendship Tree. The garden flourished with flowers of every color, a blend of wildflowers and perennials that created a stunning tapestry around the mural and pavilion.

On the day of the grand opening, the entire town gathered in the park to celebrate. The atmosphere was festive, filled with laughter, music, and the scent of flowers from the newly planted garden. Children ran around, their laughter ringing through the air, while adults marveled at the changes and shared memories of the Friendship Tree. The friends felt a deep sense of accomplishment as they looked around at what they had helped create. Their vision had grown far beyond what they had imagined, shaped by the community's love and dedication.

As the sun began to set, casting a warm golden glow over the park, a ceremony was held to officially open the new area around the Friendship Tree. Elara, who had been chosen to speak on behalf of the original friends, stepped forward. She stood under the tree, looking out at the familiar faces and feeling a surge of gratitude. She spoke of the tree's history, of the lessons it had taught them, and of the friendships that had blossomed around it. Her words were filled with love and pride, and as she finished, the crowd erupted in applause, their voices filled with joy and appreciation.

After the ceremony, people gathered around the plaques, reading the stories and memories etched into them. Each plaque held a unique piece of the tree's legacy, a story of love, friendship, resilience, or growth. People took turns sharing their own memories, adding to the collective tapestry of experiences that surrounded the tree. The pavilion quickly became a gathering place, a place where people could sit and talk, sharing stories and connecting with one another. The Friendship Tree stood at the heart of it all, its branches stretching wide as if embracing everyone who came near.

For Samira, Leo, Elara, and Liam, the experience was a profound reminder of the power of community. They realized that the tree's legacy was no longer just their own; it belonged to everyone who had come to love it, everyone who had left a piece of themselves in the park. The tree had grown into something larger than they had ever imagined, a symbol of unity, love, and hope that would endure for generations to come.

Chapter 24: Seeds of the Future

The Friendship Tree had become a cornerstone of the town, but over time, it had also come to represent a vision of the future—a reminder to every generation that kindness, unity, and growth were principles that could shape a better world. It was not only a symbol of friendship but of the interconnectedness of the people who visited the park. Parents told their children stories about it, schools organized visits where teachers shared its history, and town events often took place in its shadow. It had become not just a part of the landscape but a part of the community's identity, something they proudly shared with visitors from near and far.

As the years passed, the friends who had once planted the tree became mentors and teachers themselves, passing down the lessons they had learned to the next generation. Samira, who had grown into an artist with a passion for community-driven projects, proposed an idea to the town council: a time capsule filled with messages, dreams, and artifacts that represented the values of the Friendship Tree. The idea was simple but powerful—a way for future generations to connect with the past, to feel the enduring love and unity the tree symbolized, and to contribute their own hopes and visions for the future.

The town council embraced the idea enthusiastically, recognizing that a time capsule would create a tangible link between generations, a way to share the spirit of the tree with those yet to come. With the council's support, Samira organized a series of workshops at the town's community center where people of all ages could come together to write letters, draw pictures, and create small artifacts for the capsule. She wanted everyone, from young children to the elderly, to have the opportunity to contribute something meaningful.

The workshops were filled with laughter, stories, and creativity. Children drew pictures of the tree, capturing it in their unique styles, with some imagining it in ways that only a child's mind could envision—towering over a colorful village, hosting tea parties in its branches, or sheltering animals from every corner of the forest. Teens wrote poems and letters, expressing their hopes and dreams, their thoughts about friendship, and the ways the tree had inspired them. Many adults wrote letters, reflecting on the role the tree had played in their lives or sharing their wishes for a world built on kindness and compassion. Elders brought small keepsakes, like a piece of fabric, a ribbon, or even a handwritten recipe, each item holding a piece of their personal histories and the wisdom they hoped to pass down.

Samira marveled at the diversity of contributions. The time capsule was becoming a beautiful collection of memories and dreams, a testament to the ways people could come together and share pieces of their lives. She carefully cataloged each item, writing down notes about their significance so that future generations would understand the meaning behind every piece. She saw her own friends in the contributions of others—the creativity, love, hope, and determination that they had shared over the years. The time capsule, like the Friendship Tree itself, was becoming a reflection of the town's collective spirit.

One afternoon, as Samira was organizing the contributions, Elara joined her. The two friends sat together, looking through the letters and items people had submitted. Elara held a note written by a young girl who dreamed of becoming an astronaut, her words filled with excitement about exploring the stars. Another letter, written by an elderly man, shared memories of his own childhood, describing how the tree had been a place of comfort during difficult times. Each story and item represented a unique perspective, a different piece of the community's heart, and Samira and Elara were deeply moved by the love and thoughtfulness poured into each contribution.

When the time capsule was ready, the town organized a special ceremony to bury it near the base of the Friendship Tree. On the day of the event, people gathered from all over, filling the park with a joyful energy. Families, friends, and neighbors stood side by side, each of them united by their shared connection to the tree. The crowd was filled with familiar faces—children who had grown up playing under the tree, elders who had watched it grow, and newcomers who had recently discovered its significance. Everyone had come to honor the tree and to be a part of something bigger than themselves, something that would last far beyond their own lives.

The ceremony began with a few words from the town's mayor, who spoke about the enduring legacy of the Friendship Tree. She shared her own memories of visiting the park as a child, of the comfort she had found in its shade, and of the ways it had brought people together. She spoke about the importance of the time capsule, about how it would serve as a message to future generations, a reminder of the values that had shaped the town. Her words were met with applause, and as she finished, she invited Samira to say a few words.

Samira stepped forward, her heart pounding with a mix of excitement and gratitude. She looked out at the crowd, seeing her friends, her family, and the faces of people who had come to mean so much to her. She spoke about the journey of the Friendship Tree, from the day it had been planted to the present, describing the lessons it had taught her and the love it had inspired. She thanked everyone for their contributions, for the memories and dreams they had shared, and for helping to create a legacy that would live on for generations. She emphasized that the time capsule was not just a collection of items, but a gift of hope, a way to connect with the future, and a reminder that kindness and unity were timeless values.

When Samira finished speaking, the crowd gathered around the time capsule, each person taking a moment to place a hand on it, to whisper a silent wish or thought. Some people closed their eyes, their faces reflecting a quiet reverence, while others smiled, their expressions filled with pride and joy. The capsule was carefully lowered into the ground, and as the first shovelful of soil was placed over it, people began to clap, their applause a celebration of everything the capsule represented.

After the ceremony, people lingered around the Friendship Tree, sharing stories and memories with one another. They talked about the time capsule and what it meant to them, imagining the future generations who would one day open it, who would read their letters, see their drawings, and feel the love that had gone into every piece. It was a profound moment, a connection across time that filled the air with a sense of unity and purpose.

As the day turned to evening, families gathered near the mural for one last activity. Elara had arranged for a few large blank canvases to be set up, inviting people to paint their own visions of the future. Children dipped their brushes into paint, creating colorful scenes of what they imagined the tree and park might look like years from now. Teenagers and adults added their own touches, some painting symbols of peace, others drawing images of friends and family gathered under the tree. The canvases became a collaborative masterpiece, a vision of the future shaped by the love and hope of everyone who had come to celebrate the tree.

Before leaving, Samira, Elara, Leo, and Liam gathered under the tree with their families. They stood in silence for a few moments, each of them reflecting on the journey they had taken, the memories they had made, and the legacy they had created. They knew that this was not an ending but a beginning, that the tree's legacy would continue to grow, nourished by the love and dreams of everyone who visited it.

As they left the park that evening, each of them felt a deep sense of peace, knowing that the Friendship Tree would continue to be a source of inspiration, a place where people could come to reflect, connect, and find comfort. They knew that the time capsule would be a message of hope, a reminder to future generations that kindness and unity were powerful forces, capable of bridging distances and building communities. The tree had grown from a single sapling into a towering presence, but its roots went deeper than anyone could see, reaching into the hearts of everyone who had been touched by its story.

Chapter 25: The Tree's Endless Reach

Years had passed since the Friendship Tree first took root in the park, and its story had grown beyond what anyone could have ever imagined. The tree was now massive, its branches arching high above the park, providing shade to all who sat beneath it. The mural, filled with colors and symbols contributed by people from all backgrounds, stood nearby, still vivid and expanding as each new visitor added their touch. The garden flourished with flowers and plants that had been lovingly tended, each one contributing to the tree's story and connecting generations.

The tree and the area surrounding it had become a place of pilgrimage for those seeking comfort, joy, or simply a quiet moment to reflect. It had been written about in local newspapers, featured in magazines, and spoken about on radio programs, drawing visitors from nearby towns and cities. The time capsule buried near its roots was a constant reminder of the town's dedication to preserving the values of kindness, unity, and friendship. It held pieces of the past that waited patiently to be uncovered by future generations, a testament to the legacy that had grown from a single act of planting.

For the original group of friends, the tree was a reminder of their shared roots, a place that had witnessed the many stages of their lives. They each made time to visit the tree, even as they continued to grow and evolve. Elara, Samira, Leo, and Liam had all followed unique paths, but they found comfort in the knowledge that the tree was a constant in their lives. It had become a touchstone, a reminder of their youth, of the lessons they had learned, and of the bonds they had formed. No matter how far they traveled or how much they changed, the tree was always there, waiting to welcome them back.

One autumn afternoon, Elara found herself back in town for a brief visit. The air was crisp, and the leaves on the tree had turned a fiery shade of red and orange, creating a vibrant canopy that looked almost magical. She walked through the park, taking in the familiar sights, memories flooding her mind with every step. She paused by the tree, admiring the additions that had been made to the garden and the circle of mementos left by people who had come to love the tree. She felt a sense of peace wash over her, knowing that the tree was thriving and that its story was still being written.

As she sat beneath the tree, she noticed a group of children nearby, laughing and playing in the fallen leaves. They were the age she and her friends had been when they first planted the tree, and their laughter reminded her of the games they had once played in the park. One of the children, a young girl with bright eyes and a curious expression, approached her, looking at the tree with a mixture of awe and excitement. Elara smiled and motioned for her to come closer, sensing that the girl had questions.

"Is this the Friendship Tree?" the girl asked, her voice filled with wonder.

Elara nodded, her smile warm. "Yes, it is," she replied. "A long time ago, my friends and I planted this tree together. We wanted it to be a symbol of friendship, kindness, and unity."

The girl's eyes widened, and she looked at the tree with a newfound sense of reverence. "That's amazing," she whispered, reaching out to touch the rough bark. "Do you think it remembers you?"

Elara laughed softly, touched by the girl's innocence. "In a way, I think it does," she said. "Every person who visits, every story shared under its branches, becomes a part of the tree's memory. It carries all of those moments in its roots, its branches, and its leaves."

The girl was silent for a moment, her small hand resting on the tree as if trying to feel the memories within it. She looked up at Elara, her expression serious. "Will it remember me too?"

Elara nodded. "Absolutely. Every person who comes here becomes a part of its story, just like you. You can add your own story to the tree by leaving something here, something that represents you."

THE FRIENDSHIP TREE

The girl's face lit up, and she quickly ran back to her friends, whispering excitedly about the tree. Elara watched as the children gathered, discussing what they might leave behind, each of them eager to become a part of the tree's legacy. She felt a deep sense of joy, knowing that the tree's message was still reaching new hearts, still inspiring love and unity.

As she sat there, other people approached, some to sit quietly, others to admire the tree and its surroundings. A few elderly residents joined her, each of them sharing stories of the tree's impact on their lives. One woman spoke about how she had met her best friend under the tree's branches, while another man talked about how he brought his grandchildren to the park every Sunday, sharing stories of his own childhood memories tied to the tree.

As the sun began to set, casting a warm golden glow over the park, Samira, Leo, and Liam arrived. They had heard that Elara was in town and had come to see her and to spend time by the tree. The four friends embraced, their laughter filling the air, just as it had years ago. They sat together under the tree, catching up, sharing stories of their lives, and reminiscing about their shared past. Each of them carried memories of the tree that were unique and personal, but together, they created a beautiful mosaic of moments, a testament to the friendship that had blossomed under its branches.

They sat for hours, sharing dreams, goals, and memories, talking about how the tree had shaped their lives and the lives of so many others. They spoke about the time capsule buried nearby, about the hopes they had for the future, and about the generations that would one day sit where they were sitting, feeling the same connection to the tree. They knew that, while they may not always be able to visit, the tree's legacy would endure, carried forward by everyone who came to know it.

As the sky darkened, Elara suggested they each leave one final memento at the base of the tree, something that would symbolize their gratitude and their connection to the tree. They agreed, each of them finding a small item that held personal significance. Elara left a small notebook filled with reflections and lessons she had learned over the years, hoping that it would inspire others to find wisdom in their own journeys. Samira added a small paintbrush, a symbol of her creativity and the beauty she had found in community art. Leo placed a compass, a nod to his adventurous spirit and the paths he had taken. And Liam left a small carved leaf, representing his love for nature and his commitment to preserving it.

They arranged their items carefully, adding them to the circle of mementos that had grown over the years, a reminder that they were part of something much larger than themselves. As they stood together, they felt a sense of peace, knowing that their legacy was woven into the roots of the tree, carried forward by the community that had come to love it.

Before they left, they gathered in a circle, holding hands and sharing a moment of silence. They knew that this may be the last time they would all be together under the tree, but they also knew that their friendship would endure, rooted in the love and memories they had shared. The tree had become more than just a symbol; it was a part of them, a living embodiment of the values they held dear.

As they walked away, they looked back at the tree, its branches silhouetted against the evening sky. It stood tall and strong, a beacon of hope and unity, a reminder that love and friendship were the true roots of life. They knew that the tree would continue to inspire others, to be a place of connection, and to carry their story forward.

Don't miss out!

Visit the website below and you can sign up to receive emails whenever Isaac Lewis publishes a new book. There's no charge and no obligation.

https://books2read.com/r/B-A-ILLVC-LSOIF

BOOKS2READ

Connecting independent readers to independent writers.

Did you love *The Friendship Tree*? Then you should read *Khalil's Clay Creations*[1] by Eli Turner!

[2]

Khalil's Clay Creations follows the artistic journey of a young boy, Khalil, who discovers the beauty of self-expression through pottery. Alongside his friends and family, Khalil learns to embrace his unique style, celebrate cultural diversity, explore sustainability, and find calm and healing in his art. As Khalil grows, he learns that art can be a bridge connecting people, healing hearts, and building communities. This beautifully illustrated children's book encourages young readers to find joy in creativity, honor diverse perspectives, and nurture kindness and empathy. Ideal for ages 5-10, this story celebrates art, friendship, and the beauty of individuality.

---

1. https://books2read.com/u/47qJaq

2. https://books2read.com/u/47qJaq

About the Publisher

Whimsy Tales Press is a creative powerhouse devoted to publishing exceptional children's books that spark joy, imagination, and lifelong learning. With a mission to inspire young minds, the company crafts stories that celebrate diversity, kindness, and the magic of discovery. Whimsy Tales Press collaborates with passionate authors and illustrators to bring captivating characters and enchanting worlds to life. From heartwarming bedtime tales to empowering adventures, every book is designed to entertain while fostering empathy and curiosity. Committed to excellence and inclusivity, Whimsy Tales Press ensures that each story leaves a lasting impression, encouraging children to dream big and believe in endless possibilities.